A DAY TO FIGHT

JAMES HUNT

he interior of the conference room was bland. There were no pictures on the gray walls, no windows. Plastic chairs lined the walls, and a square table sat in the center where four seats were located. The room was illuminated by candles that provided an occult atmosphere, which many would argue was exactly the kind of meeting that was about to take place.

The door opened, and a stream of men entered, all of them dressed in tactical gear. Their uniforms were mismatched, but one symbol united them, which they wore with a hateful pride. On each shoulder was a bastardized version of the American flag.

At first glance, it looked normal, but a closer look revealed the swastika symbol on the blue patch where the stars should have been located. The official symbol of The New Order.

Nervous energy filled the air as the men filled the empty chairs. Everyone was eager for the latest news on the war efforts.

No official ranks had been given within The New Order, but the three men who sat at the table in the center of the room were held in high regard.

Tom Watts, Vincent Delgado, and Mark Riker. Each of them brought a level of cunning and savagery to their mission. They had laid the foundation for the organization and were integral in the planning of the EMP strike and subsequent militant attacks around the country.

Before joining The New Order, they had been wondering souls, lost and without purpose, just like the rest of the men in the room. But one man had brought them together. The one man whose chair had yet to be filled.

What started as a conversation in a basement almost ten years ago had finally come to fruition, and they were one step closer to realizing their ultimate goal. And none of them had sacrificed more than Mark Riker.

Mark had been the first disciple the supreme leader had found. He had been handpicked and molded into the supreme leader's most trusted advisor and military leader. And while he showed no outward appearance of fear, inside, he was barely holding it together.

Mark's last mission had been the most difficult of his tenure with The New Order. Harder than the detonation of the EMP, more strenuous than the endless fighting that had occurred in its aftermath. But keeping the truth a secret, he had learned, was more dangerous than speaking it aloud.

The supreme leader stepped through the door, and every fighter stood, showing their respect. He entered alone, as he always did.

The supreme leader found his chair but didn't sit at first. He glanced around the room, pausing to look each man in the eye. The supreme leader wasn't a large man; nothing about him appeared extraordinary at first glance. He was of average height and weight. He wasn't much of a fighter. He didn't have the greatest military mind. By many respects he was unremarkable, the kind of man that blended into the background.

But he had a way with words. And he was skilled at reaching into the minds of those who society had cast aside, and over the years, he had developed a following who had become his zealots for his twisted vision of the future.

A future that was becoming frighteningly close to reality.

"The night is long, but the dawn is bright," the supreme leader said.

The New Order's mantra was parroted back to the supreme leader, and when he sat down, the rest of his men followed suit.

"Conviction is something I've always preached about," the supreme leader said. "Without conviction, we are lost and wandering souls finding meaning in the meaningless and purpose in ambiguity."

Mark struggled to sit still, and despite the fact that the supreme leader wasn't even looking at him, he was certain he saw Mark fidgeting.

"I have been straightforward from the very beginning about our mission and the likelihood of success," the supreme leader said. "The longer we are engaged in modern warfare with our enemy, the less likely our victory becomes a reality. We do not benefit from prolonged warfare. We don't have the men, and we don't have the time. The EMP was simply a starting point for us, but we all knew this country's military would regroup. It's only a matter of time before they have air superiority and all of their tanks and missiles back online. Once that type of weaponry is unleashed against us, it will not matter how much food we have or how many automatic rifles we collected, or the stockpile of bullets in our coffers. The only way we win is through the complete annihilation of the central nervous system of our enemy. We strike at the heart with precision and purpose." He closed his hand into a fist, and every eye in the room was drawn to it.

That fist was a symbol of strength to the men in the room, just as the bastardized flag emblazoned on their shoulders.

"Our conviction is the only weapon the enemy cannot take away from us," the supreme leader said. "It is the sharpest tool in our arsenal, and it can propel us through any hardship. And make no mistake that hardship is on the horizon."

While the supreme leader spoke of conviction, all Mark could think about was how he had shown his enemy mercy. The past he had thought was buried had resurfaced, and with it came a conflict he had avoided over a decade before.

"Bring him in!" the supreme leader shouted.

The door opened, and a man was dragged inside with a bag over his head, escorted by two of their fighters. The prisoner was dropped to his knees next to the supreme leader.

Mark and the rest of the men in the room winced from the man's stench. It was a mixture of sour and rot, like the dead animals Mark had seen left on the side of the road when he had lived in the mountains. He recalled a deer that had been hit by a car. Smaller critters had eaten away at the animal's belly, leaving nothing but legs and ribs. Ants crawled around the eyes and the tongue, slowly devouring the tender flesh. And as gruesome as the site was, it was the smell that stuck with Mark—the same kind of smell that was here now.

The smell of death.

"Our work is not easy," the supreme leader said, still addressing the room while everybody else stared at the shivering man with the bag over his head. "The path ahead is riddled with pitfalls and traps, sirens luring us to the rocky shoals."

The supreme leader reached over and placed his hand on the top of the man's head.

"This was one of our men," the supreme leader said. "I speak in the past tense because he is no longer one of us. He had forsaken the vows he took to see our cause through to the end." The supreme leader turned toward the traitor. "There are consequences for every action we take. And there are consequences for the secrets he has told our enemy."

The room became unsettled. Because of their relatively small size, The New Order relied heavily on deception as their fighting tactic. And so far, it had been extremely successful.

"This traitor gave up the location of our command center in Johnson City," the supreme leader said. "And he has given up code we've been using as communication across the country."

Another wave of anxious murmurs rippled through the room. They had used Arabic as their code language to confuse the military that the EMP attack had been made by foreign terrorists. And if the military knew their command center, it wouldn't be long before they mobilized for an attack.

"Calm yourselves, men," the supreme leader said. "This was something I had foreseen. What this traitor hadn't realized was that I had known of his breach in our trust for weeks and had been giving him false intelligence. And through my conviction, I have managed to create an opportunity for us." He brandished a knife and then held it to the man's throat. "I take no pleasure in killing a brother. But there must be consequences if we lose our way. It is imperative we retain our conviction, till our last man standing." He looked at the prisoner, who was still trembling. "You will not be the last man." He looked back to the men in the room. "But one of you will be. And if that day comes, then I want you to remember this day."

The supreme leader sliced the man's throat, and blood cascaded down the front of his shirt, soaking him in crimson. The supreme leader kept hold of the man's head until the last bits of life had drained from him and then let him collapse onto the floor.

Even after the man had died, the bag over his head was never removed. And all Mark could think about when he stared at the dead man was picturing himself underneath it.

"Remember this day, gentlemen," the supreme leader said. "We will all die. But we can make sure our deaths are more honorable than a traitor's death." He paused for a moment, letting his words marinate, and then set down the knife and proceeded with their business as if nothing had happened.

"I want our regional updates," the supreme leader said.

Tom Watts, an image of Aerian perfection, which looked harrowing in the flickering shadows of the candlelight, produced a map that showed where they had gathered their forces and other resources.

"The Northeast, Midwest, and Southeast have all reported successful missions," Tom said. "Food, water, and medical resources have been gathered and stored with our men. And local infrastructure integral to the metropolitan areas has been destroyed. However, we're still having trouble along the West Coast, but we anticipated a high level of resistance due to the number of military installations in California."

The New Order had units in every state across the country, and regional commanders were responsible for securing as many resources and destroying as much infrastructure as possible in order to cripple the local populations and render any rebuilding efforts difficult or impossible. Whoever said not to kick a dog when it was down wasn't in the business of winning wars.

The supreme leader studied the map on the small table for a few minutes and then tapped his finger on the famous Camp Lejeune.

"The military has mobilized their marines," the supreme leader said. "They're set to march west and start re-establishing order in the major cities in the state, and they are set to meet forces coming from bases stationed in Arkansas and northern Alabama. And they are to meet here, in Asheville."

Mark shifted uneasily as he stared at the map, not because of the enemy forces gathering around them but because of a small town outside of Asheville. It was where he had grown up and where he had visited recently on a mission for the supreme leader.

"It's a pincer move," Vincent Delgado said, who was their lead military strategist, and then he looked up from the map and to the supreme leader with his catlike eyes. His entire demeanor was catlike, sanguine at first, but ready to strike at a moment's notice. "You fed the traitor information because you *wanted* the military to mobilize these troops?"

"The forces from the west are already on the move and are set to arrive in Asheville by today," the supreme leader said. "But they're simply setting up a command post, and the rest of the forces from Camp Lejeune are meeting them there in a few days. If we can move the bulk of our forces in Johnson City and meet these western forces coming from Texas and Alabama, we could take them out before they have a chance to unite with the marines from the east," the supreme leader said.

"We would have to get the word out to our camps quickly in order to get everybody in position," Tom said. "Are those the orders, sir?"

Everybody waited for the supreme leader to speak, and it was so quiet that Mark could hear his heartbeat.

"Yes," the supreme leader answered. "Where are we with our weapons program?"

Vincent Delgado leaned forward, pressing his forearms against the edge of the table as he clasped his hands together. He was a shrewd military man, someone who studied the greats of the past but had

9

never had any practical experience. But that was proving unimportant.

"Our work camps are starting to pick up steam," Vincent said. "The engineers and scientists we drafted into our service were resistant at first, but they've… come around."

"Excellent," the supreme leader said. "Let's try to have something ready for these soldiers who think they've managed to one-up us."

Finally, the supreme leader swiveled toward Mark. "Status update on our next phase?" the supreme leader asked.

Mark cleared his throat. "We are still on schedule, sir. The scientists at the camps have been working diligently. And with the pieces we dug up from the silo in the mountains, we've been told that the engineers have everything they need to make the weapon."

"Except for the final two pieces," the supreme leader said.

Mark quickly nodded. "Yes, sir. Except for those final two pieces. But the first should be completed today."

"Excellent," the supreme leader said, and then he eyed the map and circled Washington, DC. "Too long this seat of power has gone unchecked. But the fallout from our next move will be the final spear into the heart of the old world." He looked up to the rest of the room. "You all have followed me because you understand the new world we are looking to build. Stay the course, men. The night is long, but the dawn is bright."

Again the mantra was parroted in the room, and the men were dismissed. But after everyone had left, Mark lingered behind, and when they were alone, Mark closed the door.

"Is there something on your mind, Marcus?" the supreme leader asked.

Mark was caught staring at the blood of the traitor on the floor. He cleared his throat. "Sir, there is something I need to tell you."

"Speak," the supreme leader said.

A cold sense of dread started in the pit of Mark's stomach and spread out through his extremities. "I lied to you about the results of my mission from Charlotte." He forced himself to hold the supreme leader's gaze. "There were survivors. I did not kill the man I had been sent to find."

The supreme leader remained quiet.

"The man I found, the one who had caused trouble at one of our prisoner camps, he was my brother, sir." Mark's voice caught in his throat, and he hated himself for the weakness he was showing. "I could have killed him, but I didn't." He straightened up and lifted his chin. "I am willing to accept the consequences of my actions, sir."

The supreme leader nodded and then stood. "Our work is not easy. The sacrifices that we make in order to build the world we wish to see have been great." He walked to Mark and placed his hand on his shoulder. "I know the history you have with your brother. I understand your hesitation." He leaned closer. "But you must go back to finish the work you started."

"Sir?" Mark asked.

The supreme leader gestured back to the map on the table. "Asheville, your home, will become a pivotal turning point in our fight. If we can cripple the enemy forces there, catch them off guard, then it will buy us time for our ultimate goal." He turned back to Mark. "I want you to lead these forces."

Mark shook his head, confused. "Sir, I lied to you. I betrayed your trust—"

"You have been with me from the beginning," the supreme leader said. "Your conviction is still strong, but you must erase the doubts that plague you. Return to your home, and finish what you set out to do." He gripped the back of Mark's head. "When all of this is done, the scholars will write our history. Decades from now, we will be the ones they build statues for. We will be the people who are remembered." He looked up and stared at Mark. "But only if we stay the course."

"Yes, sir," Mark said, his voice stronger and steadier than the rest of his body.

"Good," the supreme leader said and then walked back over to the map and smiled as he pressed his thumb against the dot that represented Washington, DC. "We will level the entire city with a single blast, built from the very weapons of destruction they believed would keep them safe." He glanced down at the blood stain on the floor. "Send somebody in here to clean this up."

The supreme leader left the room, and once he was gone, Mark collapsed back into his chair. He broke out in a thick sheen of sweat, and he could smell his own fear and desperation over that of the dead man. He had been given a second chance. But that second chance would come at the cost of his brother's life.

But killing Ben Riker would be more difficult than Mark could imagine.

2

―――――――――

*B*en Riker made sure to keep the horses at a modest pace, not wanting to tire the last two remaining animals at their disposal.

Ben adjusted himself in the saddle, one hand on the reins, the other kept idle on his right thigh in case he needed to quickly reach for his pistol. The past two months had caused his jet-black hair to become disheveled, his beard was growing thicker, and he had lost some weight, but the astute green eyes remained unchanged.

Ben glanced behind him at the horse he had kept on a lead, which carried the body Ben had brought with him on his journey. The body was wrapped in a tarp and hung limply over the saddle.

Buzzards circled overhead against the blue morning sky, the birds catching the scent of death. It was just one of the countless casualties in the war that had raged since the EMP attack had brought the country to a standstill.

People had lost their homes, their livelihoods, and their families. The past few months had been the most difficult anyone had experienced in their lifetime. And the survivors of the first wave of attacks were still trying to piece together what had happened.

The risks involved in the shadowy collapse of the old world were great, and this journey Ben was taking was no exception. But he knew his brother better than he did the enemy, and while Ben might have won the latest battle, the war was far from over.

Ben had stuck close to the highway as a guide, but he kept to the forest to keep himself hidden as much as possible. He had grown up in these woods, knew them like his own beating heart. Any shift on the breeze could alert him to trouble, so when he heard the snap of the twig on his right, he slowed his horse.

"Easy, girl," Ben said, gently pulling on the reins.

The horse whinnied but obeyed and slowed. Ben reached for his side arm as he studied the tree line to his left. Another twig snapped, followed by a crunch of leaves, and Ben knew he wasn't alone.

"I need you to stop right there, sir," a voice said. "And I need you to keep your hands up where I can see them."

Three men emerged from the trees where Ben had heard them moving. They were dressed in military fatigues, but Ben wasn't sure just yet if that was a good sign or not.

Ben took his hand off the butt of his pistol and slowly complied with the soldier's request as he was circled and surrounded. "I was just on my way to see some of your friends."

"Is that right?" one of the soldiers asked.

"We got a body back here, Sarge," another soldier said.

"You kill him?" the sergeant asked.

"No," Ben answered. "He was a soldier in Colonel Jackson's unit. He was killed by the same people who started this fight."

"You know Colonel Jackson?" the sergeant asked, sounding surprised.

"I'm on my way to see him now," Ben answered.

"Are you a civilian?" the sergeant asked.

"Yes," Ben answered.

The sergeant was a skinny man, but his jawline looked chiseled from marble. He stared at Ben with a calculating gaze. "You know, we just ran into a guy in the previous town who had a similar story to yours. Turns out he was actually part of The New Order." He examined Ben's shoulders, no doubt looking for the patch their people wore. "You know about them?"

"I do," Ben answered, sensing that the situation was turning tense.

"Hey, Sarge?" The soldier who was examining the body on the horse removed a pair of dog tags.

"Well, at least the dead soldier story checks out," the sergeant answered. "But I'm afraid that still doesn't ease my concerns, so…" He gestured down with the end of his rifle.

When Ben didn't comply, the two soldiers under the sergeant's command grabbed at his legs, but Ben swatted them away.

"Hey, easy," Ben said. "I'm coming down."

Once dismounted and disarmed, Ben marched forward with his new wardens, the horses pulled with them. "It's a waste not to ride one of them," Ben said.

"I don't like horses," the sergeant said, and then he spat. "They're too skittish for me."

Ben examined the three of them, and it looked like they been through hell. "How long have you men been roughing it?"

"Six weeks," the sergeant answered, sounding exasperated. "We've been tasked with locating all the military installations across the state and making sure everybody is still at their post."

"What you found so far?" Ben asked.

"That's classified," the sergeant answered.

"But what you've already told me isn't?" Ben asked.

The sergeant gave Ben a good look up and down. "Let's say I believe you. What are you going to speak with Colonel Jackson about?"

"We had an arrangement," Ben answered. "I was visiting to make sure our agreement was still in place."

The sergeant looked back to the dead body on the

horse. "If keeping that guy alive was a part of your arrangement, then I could have saved you the trip and told you that the deal was off."

"I also have information," Ben said.

The sergeant stopped, and everyone followed suit. "What kind of information?"

Ben wasn't sure how much he should tell the sergeant. They might all be dressed in military garb, but they could have pilfered those uniforms off of any dead soldier. It was hard to find people to trust these days.

"It's classified," Ben said.

The sergeant remained stoic for a moment and then laughed as he started walking again. "I like you, civilian. Not many people keep their sense of humor during times like these. It's good to know that you still have it."

The mood lightened after that, and Ben was still forced to walk, but the sergeant opened up a little bit more about their mission.

"Between the two of us, we should be able to end this war by next week," the sergeant said.

Ben perked up. "How?"

"We managed to turn someone on the inside of The New Order," the sergeant answered. "The details are complicated, but let's just say that we know where their command is stationed. We're putting together units that will cut the head off the snake."

"Oorah," the two soldiers behind them chanted.

"Ooo-rah," the sergeant repeated. "Take these fuckers out in one swift swoop."

"Good," Ben said. "The sooner, the better."

When they finally neared the gates of Jackson's facility, they were ordered to stop by the guards on duty. Ben's nerves got the better of him as he again doubted coming here. There was no telling how Jackson would react to the death of one of his men.

When the gates finally opened, Lieutenant Colonel Jackson was standing directly in the middle of the entrance with his hands on his hips. The colonel was a shorter man but stocky, with a very practiced thousand-yard stare. He was flanked on both sides by two soldiers. He barely had a dozen men at his disposal, but he had managed to keep his facility secure throughout the EMP strike.

"That better not be my man on the back of that horse," Jackson said.

Ben made sure to choose his next words carefully. "We need to talk."

Jackson's eye twitched, and he had a holstered pistol at his hip. "Who are your friends?"

"Sergeant Ken Tanner, sir," he answered. "My men and I were tasked to seek you out and provide you with information directly from General McGuire." The sergeant looked at Ben. "He says he has information to tell you, too."

Jackson took a deep breath. "All right then. I'll speak

to you one at a time. Sergeant, you're up first. And will someone please get Beckett off the back of that horse!"

Jackson and the sergeant departed into one of the buildings while Ben was forced to wait outside. He watched as two other soldiers removed Beckett's body from the horse. They gently laid him on the ground, unsure of what to do with him.

"I'm sorry about your friend," Ben said.

"Beckett wasn't just my friend," the soldier said. "He was my brother." He adjusted his grip on the AR-15, keeping that cold, hard stare on Ben.

Ben nodded and decided that keeping quiet was the best possible scenario for him to keep all of his teeth. But the silence that followed was almost as uncomfortable as the restraints, and Ben grew uneasy as the soldier refused to take his eye off of him.

"Did you kill him?" the soldier finally asked.

"No," Ben answered.

The soldier shifted his weight from one leg to another. "It would take balls to come back here with his body if you did. Or you might be some kind of a spy."

"I don't have the constitution to be a spy," Ben said.

The soldier grinned, but it was barely noticeable through the scowl. Still, Ben took it as a good sign.

"How many friends have you lost?" Ben asked.

The soldier kept his eyes on the ground shook his head. "Too many. And I know we are going to lose more before all this is over." The soldier looked to Ben. "Have you lost any?"

Ben thought back to the friends who followed him from the fire station. He thought of Jeff and Ali and Ted. If it weren't for Ben, then all of those people would still be alive.

"I have," Ben answered. "But I hope that in the end, I save more people than I lose."

Ben grew anxious the longer he waited outside, and when he was finally pulled inside to speak with Jackson, he was drenched with sweat from baking in the sun.

"Talk," Jackson said. "And make it quick."

Ben felt every eye in the room on him. These men were Beckett's comrades, and with this small of a unit, people were bound to have gotten close.

"We were ambushed on our way to the ranch where the radio was located," Ben said. "It was sniper fire that killed him and three of my people. The radio we were using to listen to the enemy's correspondence was destroyed, and the ranch was burned to the ground."

Jackson was silent, still gripping the pistol at his side, his body language tense. "And you expect me to just take your word for that?"

"If I was responsible for Beckett's death it would have made more sense for me to avoid coming back here," Ben answered.

"And why did you come?" Jackson asked.

"I came because I still need your help," Ben said. "And you need mine."

Jackson laughed. "I need your help? All you've done for me so far is have one of my men killed."

"There was something else I didn't tell you before," Ben said.

Jackson raised one eyebrow. "I don't think now is the time to admit that you're a liar, Ben."

"It was more of an omission," Ben replied. "The day of the EMP attacks, I captured one of the enemy combatants. He was wounded by one of my people, but I spoke to him before I returned here." Ben took a breath. "This organization, The New Order, the EMP isn't the only weapon of mass destruction they're building."

"You're telling me that these people are trying to build a bomb?" Jackson asked.

"Yes," Ben answered.

"And how did this captured enemy know this information?" Jackson asked. "What rank is he?"

"What does it matter what rank he is? They're building a nuke!" Ben answered.

Jackson clenched his jaw. "He could just be feeding you a line to save his own skin."

"Do you know what an EMP device does?" Ben asked.

"I think we all know what it does now," Jackson answered.

"All right, well, a side effect of a nuclear bomb is an EMP," Ben replied.

"You're telling me they've already nuked the country somewhere?" Jackson asked.

"I'm saying that if these people managed to build and detonate an EMP device strong enough to wipe out the entire country's grid, then it's not insane to think they would be able to add a nuclear component to their next bomb."

Jackson stiffened, and Ben saw the colonel's wheels turning behind that stoic gaze.

"The prisoner back at my camp told me his people had dug up an old missile silo in the mountains outside of Charlotte," Ben said. "They're using those old parts to build a new bomb."

"And this prisoner at your camp knows where we can find these components for the bomb?" Jackson asked.

"Yes," Ben answered.

It wasn't necessarily a lie because the truth was Ben didn't know if Abe knew the location of the other components. But if it would get Jackson to believe him, then it was worth a shot.

"I'm not lying about the bomb," Ben said.

"That remains to be seen," Jackson said, and then he motioned for Ben to join him over by a table. On it was a map of the region. "The sergeant gave me some intelligence that will cause us to relocate to Asheville, and considering that's your hometown, I'm going to keep you around."

Ben frowned. "Why Asheville?"

"That's where our forces from the west were going to be stationed for our push toward the coast." Jackson pointed back to the map. "Our marines from Camp Lejeune will be coming from the east, and we will perform our pincer move, crushing anybody in between."

Ben thought about the bomb and its effectiveness and where the enemy would try to use it. His first instinct was Washington, DC, but wiping out most of the eastern ground forces would be another favorable target.

"I want to meet with your prisoner," Jackson said.

"So you believe me?" Ben asked.

Jackson started loading ammunition into a pistol magazine and shook his head. "My job isn't to believe or not believe. I'm supposed to ensure the safety of my men and the people of the state, and if what you're telling me has a shred of truth in it, I wouldn't be doing my duty if I didn't investigate." He finished loading the bullets into the magazine. "What people believe prevails over the truth. Sophocles said that."

"You didn't strike me as a philosophical man, Colonel," Ben said.

Jackson shoved the magazine into a Glock7. "Well, I'm just full of surprises."

3

*L*iz Riker lifted the bag of wheat into the wagon with the other supplies they had gathered on the north side of Asheville. The morning sun was already burning hot, and she wiped the sweat collecting in her eyebrows before it stung her eyes.

Liz's shirt clung to her small but sturdy frame. She kept her mousy-brown hair up in a ponytail in an attempt to keep her neck cool, but her fair skin was already burning from the mid-morning sun. Her daughter, Sarah, emerged from the feed store, carrying another box, her rifle strapped over her shoulder.

"Is that the last of it?" Liz asked.

Sarah dropped the box into the wagon where it landed with a thud, nearly knocking over the other bags and supplies they had collected on their trip here. "That's it."

"I'm glad this place survived the fires," Liz said. "We

have enough seed to plant crops to get us through the winter."

"Yeah, if we can get them to grow," Sarah said. "Last time I checked, you and I weren't farmers."

Liz walked to the front of the wagon and picked up the handle. "Your father and I took a few homesteading lessons over the years. We aren't experts, but we know enough to get started."

Sarah kept her gun at the ready, the stock tucked under her shoulder as she walked next to her mother. "I guess it couldn't be that hard, right? The ground does most of the work. All we do is dig the hole and make sure it gets some water. Piece of cake."

"Exactly," Liz said. "Piece of cake."

Liz flashed a smile, but it was only a façade. She was doing her best to remain calm, but her mind was already working on their next moves. She knew that with the number of mouths they now had to feed, it would be important to be able to produce their own food. Their current food stores were limited, but they had enough to keep everyone fed for now.

"What do you think Dad is doing right now?" Sarah asked.

Liz had put on a brave face when Ben had left to speak with Colonel Jackson, but both of them had their doubts of whether or not Jackson would believe their story about what had happened to his soldier. Not to mention all of the dangers a person encountered just by walking out on the road these days.

"He should be at the facility by now," Liz answered. "And if all goes according to plan, then our alliance with the military will continue."

"Dad doesn't think anyone will believe him, does he?" Sarah asked.

That was putting it mildly. "Your father has a way of convincing people to trust him. It's how he made so many relationships with the fire department."

Sarah tilted her head to the side. "He was their boss."

"Yes, but he was more than that," Liz said, switching hands as she pulled the wagon. "Your father holds an important standing in people's minds around here. The Riker name means something to them, and they see your father as the head of that name."

Sarah was quiet for a minute. "And what about Uncle Mark?" She looked at her mother. "What do they think of him?"

Liz couldn't hide her grimace. "That man is not your uncle."

"Mom," Sarah said, stepping in front of Liz and forcing her to stop. "If there is anyone who should be mad at him, it's me. I just want to know what happened between them."

Liz knew Sarah had a point, but she didn't know the whole story. "Your father had a tumultuous relationship with his brother."

"Because of what happened after Dad's parents died?" Sarah asked.

Liz nodded. "Your uncle abandoned your father to fend for himself. He was only a boy at the time, and it was very difficult for him. They tried to reconcile ten years ago, and for a while, I thought they might work it out. But then your uncle vanished."

"Until recently," Sarah said.

Liz noted the distance in her daughter's voice. Mark Riker had kidnapped Sarah in hopes of drawing Ben's attention. It had worked, but the confrontation didn't go as planned. And while Ben managed to recover Sarah unharmed, Mark had escaped, and Ben feared his brother would return for retaliation. It was one of the reasons he had decided to return to Colonel Jackson. The kidnapping had been traumatic, even though Sarah hadn't been injured.

"If you ever need to talk to me about what happened, I'm always here," Liz said.

Sarah nodded. "I know."

Liz reached for her daughter's hand and clasped it between her own. "I'm serious, anytime."

Sarah looked at her mother, and she was suddenly a child again. "Even if it's not easy to hear?"

Liz squeezed Sarah's hands. "I can handle anything. The only thing I can't handle is you beating yourself up over something that wasn't your fault."

Sarah was long past her teenage angst phase, but she could be stubborn like her mother. And she looked more like Liz every day. They had the same hair, same fair skin, though Sarah had inherited her father's dimples. Her biological father's dimples.

"Thanks," Sarah said.

Liz let her go, and Sarah walked ahead. "Listen, when we get back, I need you to start planning the funerals," Liz said, changing the subject.

Sarah frowned. "But we've already buried them."

"We buried them because we didn't have anywhere to stash the bodies," Liz replied. "We thought it best to get them into the ground as soon as possible so the bodies would decompose. That's not something their loved ones needed to see."

"So you want to actually have some type of ceremony?" Sarah asked.

"I think it would be a good opportunity for people to properly say goodbye and for the community to pay their respects," Liz answered. "With everything that's been going on, I think people need something to grieve."

"So to lift everybody's spirits and to give the community something to look forward to, we want to throw a funeral?" Sarah asked.

"You know what I mean," Liz said.

"I guess it wouldn't hurt for people to take a moment and reflect on everything that's happened," Sarah said.

Liz thought that keeping Sarah busy would be a good thing. People needed a distraction, now more than ever.

When they finally reached the river where they would cross, Liz and Sarah started loading the supplies onto the canoes they used to ferry themselves across the water.

Once all the supplies were loaded and they had crossed the river, they began the process of pulling their goods up the final hill where the training facility was perched. It had been nothing but luck that allowed the facility to survive the fires that had ravaged most of Asheville, including their home.

The facility was enclosed by a chain-link fence complete with barbed wire wrapped over the top. In addition to the fence, there was also a large tower centered inside the property. It was used for running drills, carrying fire hoses and equipment up several flights of stairs to get the firefighters conditioned for possible scenarios of fighting fires. But it also doubled as a watchtower now that they had sought refuge in this place. The watchtower was the center of the entire facility, and it gave them a bird's-eye view of any threats heading their way. The tower was always manned with someone who could handle a sniper rifle.

The community they had built at the fire training facility had grown considerably over the past few months. What had started as a small group of about a dozen had now almost tripled in size. The increase in the population had caused a strain on their supply of food, medicine, and living space. It had also begun to put a strain on everybody's mental state. There was only so much space to go around.

But everybody was still alive, and so long as Liz could keep everybody fed, she knew that they could maintain a level of civilized discourse. Or at least, she hoped.

Liz and Sarah brought the food into the mess hall, which was the main building of the fire facility. Inside was a working kitchen and massive food coolers where they stored their goods. The coolers weren't operational because they had no power, but they still provided a central location for their supplies.

Because of the security breaches they'd had since the beginning of their occupation of the facility, Liz and Ben both made the decision to keep a person stationed at the coolers to guard the food, just to make sure no one was skimming.

"Hey, guys," Cole said.

"Hey," Sarah said coldly.

Cole was Sarah's biological father. Cole had gotten Liz pregnant in high school and then took off after Sarah was born. But the past few years, Cole had tried to become a fixture in Sarah's life. Up until the EMP, they had started to mend their relationship, but when Cole had come clean about secretly dating Liz's sister, Rachel, for the past six months, their progress had stalled.

The relationship between Cole and Rachel had been a surprise to everyone who knew them, and no one was more shocked than Sarah. And while Liz had been upset about the relationship initially, she had come to terms with it. Her sister and Cole seemed to really care about one another, and it was the first time she had seen either of them really commit to anything.

Cole blushed, still embarrassed by his daughter's cold shoulder, and he stepped aside as Sarah started carrying the boxes into the storage locker.

"You want to give us a hand?" Liz asked when she noticed Cole just standing around.

"Oh, yeah, of course." Cole set down his rifle, and then the three of them set up an assembly line, feeding the boxes of food and grain into the storage locker. "Oh, did you see the chickens?"

Liz frowned. "Chickens?"

"Yeah, the Percy's found some chickens on their scouting mission today," Cole answered. "Isn't that great?"

"Yeah," Liz answered, but she didn't share the same level of enthusiasm as Cole when it came to the Percy family.

They had a history with her husband, one that was even darker than Ben's history with his brother.

"Where did they find them?" Sarah asked.

Cole perked up, eager to pick up a conversation with his daughter. "I think they said they found them north of the woods. There was an old barn they were sheltering inside."

"Good thing we have grain and corn," Liz said.

"Yeah," Cole answered. "All we need now is a pig for some bacon, and we'd have a nice breakfast." He laughed, but neither Sarah nor Liz reciprocated.

Once they finished unloading, Liz pulled Sarah to the side. "Go easy on him, will you?"

Sarah kept her voice low. "I'm not as mad as I was. But I still want him to think it, you know?"

Liz smirked. "Trust me. I know."

"Right," Sarah said, and she cleared her throat. "Well, I should get everyone ready for that... funeral." She walked away, leaving Liz and Cole alone.

"Is there anything I can do to make her forgive me?" Cole asked.

"It's just going to take some time," Liz answered.

Cole nodded, disappointed, but he dropped the subject. Once the rest of the supplies were loaded, Liz left the main building and was intercepted by Susan and Kurt Johnson with their newborn.

"Hey, guys," Liz said, glad to see a friendly face. "How are you?"

Susan had recently given birth right after the EMP's detonation. Their child was born healthy but recently had a bout of neonatal sepsis; however, they had managed to find some antibiotics, and the baby was doing much better. It was a rare victory considering the times.

"We're doing great," Susan answered even though there was no sign of a smile. Both parents looked exhausted from their efforts of handling the infant, and Liz didn't miss those sleepless nights.

"We actually wanted to talk to you about something," Kurt said. "With my leg getting a little better and me being able to walk around, I want to start pulling my weight."

"And even though I'm still dealing with the baby, I want you to know that I can help out with whatever you need here at the facility," Susan said. "After what your family has done for us, we want to repay the hospitality and the kindness."

"That's great," Liz said, and she racked her brain for any jobs the pair could handle in their current state. "We're actually trying to have a small ceremony for Marty's wife, Ali, and Ted Bartman."

"That's terrible what happened to them," Susan said, their newborn cooing in her arms.

"I can't believe those people managed to come back here," Kurt said. "Anyone associated with The New Order are animals."

Liz nodded. The fact that it had been Ben's brother who had attacked them had been kept a secret from the rest of the community. Only the immediate family knew that Ben's brother was part of The New Order that had declared war against the country.

"We'd be happy to help with the memorial," Susan said.

"Great," Liz said. "I'll send my daughter over to your portable to fill you in on the details."

Kurt and Susan again thanked Liz for her help, and as they walked away, the baby started to grow fussy, probably ready for another feeding.

But after the Johnson family had gone, Liz felt the guilt wash over her. She and Ben had assured everyone that they were safe here, but the truth was, they were still very much at risk. She had been hesitant to lie, but she understood the necessity.

The lie was needed for stability. They were already walking a fine line of keeping the peace, and it would take only the smallest incident to push everyone over the edge and throw their community into chaos.

* * *

ARMED with a small notebook and a pencil she had dug up from one of the offices in the main building, Sarah started making the rounds to see who was willing to help with Ali and Ted's memorial service.

It had been a few weeks since Ted and Ali's death. Sarah disagreed with her mother over having a service so long after they had buried the bodies, but she understood what her mother was trying to do. It was important for everyone to honor those we had lost, especially now.

The world had been turned upside down, and it was important for people to remain in touch with their humanity. Paying homage to the dead allowed some of that civility to return.

JAMES HUNT

Once Sarah had finished speaking with Kurt and Susan Johnson, shouting over the piercing screams of their newborn son, the only person left for Sarah to talk to was Marty Schwartz and his two daughters.

Sarah had put off speaking with Marty because she knew he was still taking his wife's death incredibly hard. And it didn't help matters with Marty blaming her adopted father, Ben, for Ali's death. Marty had isolated himself and his children over the past few weeks, but she could still feel his icy demeanor whenever they crossed paths in the facility.

Sarah took a breath before she knocked on Marty's door. When the door opened, it was Marty's daughter, Isabel, who answered, and Sarah was slightly relieved.

"Hey, Izzy," Sarah said. "Is your dad here?"

Isabel nodded and kept her voice down to a whisper. "He's sleeping."

Sarah looked past Isabel and into the dark portable. The interior was a mess, filled with empty food packaging, and there was a slight stench of body odor radiating from the inside. Not that everybody smelled like roses these days, but this was particularly strong.

"Okay," Sarah said. "You need anything?"

Isabel shook her head. "I'm okay. But it would be nice to go outside and play for a little bit."

Sarah's heart ached for the kid. As hard as Marty was taking his wife's passing, his daughters had also lost their mother. "Why don't you grab your sister and go outside and play for a little bit," Sarah said.

Isabel's eyes immediately lit up. She smiled and hurried inside to grab her sister, Maya. The girl looked like she'd been sleeping and rubbed her eyes. She squinted out into the late morning sunlight.

"Easy," Maya said. "I'm still tired."

Isabel practically yanked her sister outside. "It's so nice out."

Sarah was about to tell the girls not to venture too far, but before she had a chance, an angry voice bellowed from inside the portable.

"Girls, get back in here now!"

Marty emerged from the back of the darkened interior. Half of his face was still shadowed in darkness, but the small sliver of expression Sarah caught was enough to make her retreat a few steps.

The girls stopped halfway down the steps. It was Isabel who turned around, pleading with her father. "But it's so nice outside. And Maya and I are so bored."

Marty stood in the doorway. His hair was disheveled, his face crawling with a wiry black beard. His clothes looked like they had been slept in for at least a week. His complexion was pale and waxy. And the dark circles beneath his eyes made every expression more sinister. "Go back inside," Marty said.

Isabel led her sister back into the portable, both of their heads down.

"I'm sorry," Sarah said. "I didn't mean—"

"I don't care what you meant," Marty said. "I don't want you talking to my children or giving them

instructions to do anything. They are not your responsibility."

"Mr. Schwartz," Sarah said, speaking as respectfully
as she could, "I'm incredibly sorry for the loss of your
wife. I knew Ali from my visits at the fire station and
every time you guys came over for dinner. She was a
wonderful person. And this world is a far darker place
without her." "

"I don't need your condolences," Marty said. "And I
don't need you thinking that you know what's best for
my family."

"No, I'm not trying to step on anyone's toes," Sarah
said. "I just came here to tell you about a memorial that
we're holding in Ali's honor. We would like you and the
girls to attend, and if you'd like, you could say a few
words."

Sarah didn't know if Marty was going to scream at
her or cry, but when he finally spoke, he was struggling
to remain calm.

"I don't have anything else to say about what
happened to my wife," Marty said. "I don't want any
memorial. And I don't want your family using my
wife's death as some rallying cry for the community."

"Mr. Schwartz—" the door was slammed in her face
before Sarah could finish. She stood there for a
moment, staring at the closed door, listening to the
girls whisper to her father about how they wanted to
go outside.

Sarah half expected Mr. Schwartz to be just as

angry and forceful with his daughters as he had been with her, but he was incredibly calm and quiet as he spoke to them. It wasn't the tone of a man who was a danger to himself or his family but of someone who needed to remain in control of what small measures he could take to keep his family safe.

Sarah stepped off of the front porch and walked away. She had never seen Mr. Schwartz so upset, but considering the circumstances, it was understandable. She considered letting him cool off a bit and come back to try again, but she wasn't sure how far she should push her luck. The man looked like he was already on edge, and there was only so much punishment one person's psyche could take.

"Sarah!"

Sarah looked up from her clipboard and saw Rachel jogging toward her. She had been avoiding her aunt because of the situation between her and Cole. She should have known better than to think she could have avoided her forever. "Hey."

Rachel smiled. "I'm glad I caught up with you. I've been meaning to talk to you."

Sarah's aunt had never been one to shy away from a bold confrontation, something she always attributed to her red hair. Rachel and Sarah's mother didn't look much alike, and they didn't act alike either.

"What's up?" Sarah asked.

"I know Cole told you about our relationship," Rachel said.

It was rare for Rachel to show signs of remorse or regret. She'd always been the kind of woman who enjoyed living life on the edge. She was a risktaker, but as Sarah saw her aunt flush with embarrassment and avoid eye contact, she knew just how difficult this was for her.

"We should've told you," Rachel said. "But you have to understand that it wasn't just your father's decision to keep it a secret from you. It was mine as well. So, if you're going to be mad at him, you need to be mad at me."

"I am mad at you," Sarah said. "You kept this a secret from me for six months. While we were living together!" She was yelling, but the anger felt false because it had already run its course. "But I know the both of you were trying to protect me in case it didn't work out."

Rachel nodded. "We thought it best that if we ended things that it was better that you never knew something had existed at all."

"So, it's serious then?" Sarah asked.

Rachel smiled, brightening her expression. "Yes. Very serious."

Sarah knew that staying angry with both of them wasn't going to help matters. It was time to move on. "I'm over it. Really. Even though I still think you should have told me what was going on, I understand the secrecy."

A sound that was half-relief and half-happiness escaped Rachel's throat. She reached for Sarah's hand

and squeezed it firmly. "Thank you," Rachel said. "Your father and I, when we first got together, we thought it was a mistake. We were both prepared to end it, for you, for your mother, for the whole family. We understood the risk we were taking in us coming together. And you and Cole were becoming so close, I didn't want to ruin that."

"You really love him?" Sarah asked.

Rachel wiped away a tear, and for once, she did not downplay the emotions she was feeling. "I do."

"I'm happy for you," Sarah said.

Rachel lunged toward Sarah and wrapped her in a big hug. "Thank you. I didn't realize how much I needed to hear that from you." She kissed Sarah's cheek. "Anytime you need to talk, I'm always here. You know that."

"I know," Sarah said. "And if I'm being honest, I've missed our late-night chats."

Sarah had been living with Rachel while she attended college in Charlotte. The pair had grown very close, almost like a pair of sisters. Rachel had always been the fun one in the family. Sarah could remember when she was little and how Rachel had always looked so glamorous and fabulous, like a movie star. Rachel was a stark contrast to her mother, who was fun but not as flamboyant.

And right on cue, Rachel hooked her arm through Sarah's and pulled her close. "I know, and there has been so much happening to talk about. The first thing

I'd like to discuss with you is the fact that I haven't had a decent glass of wine in the months. I'd like to speak with the hotel sommelier about broadening the options here at the resort."

Sarah laughed, and it felt good to be talking with her aunt again. It was good just to be laughing. It made her feel normal again. And these days, normal was in short supply.

* * *

"AND YOU JUST FOUND THEM in the woods?" Liz asked, studying the chickens pecking the ground in the makeshift pen they had created for the animals.

Jane Percy placed her hands on her hips and cocked her head to the side. She was a wiry, petite woman, but much stronger than she looked with a mouth that didn't hold back. "Look, Liz, it wasn't like I stole them from a store. They were wandering around in the woods, and I know that we're looking to become more sustainable with our food stores. It was a no-brainer to gather them up and bring them here. Is that so hard to believe?"

Liz didn't immediately answer, and she knew that Jane took the moment of silence as a slight against her. The Percy and the Riker families had gotten off to a rocky start, but everything had been fairly peaceful for the past few weeks. Liz wanted to keep it that way.

"No," Liz answered. "We could really use fresh eggs

once they start laying. I managed to pull some grain from one of the food stores that survived the fires. The chickens won't need much to survive. And you even managed to find a rooster."

"You need both if you want eggs," Jane said. "Or is that talk too vulgar for someone like you?"

Liz dismissed the comment. "If you and your family would like to handle the maintenance of the chickens, I think that would be very helpful, and of course—"

"Liz!" Her name was barked from across the compound and with a level of anger and resentment that caused everyone in the vicinity to spin around.

Marty Schwartz marched toward Liz and Jane, arms rigid at his side. It was clear he was angry and even more clear about where that anger was directed.

"Marty—" Liz started but was cut short when Marty shoved a long, meaty finger in her face.

"I don't want your daughter, or anyone else for that matter, coming around my portable and checking on my kids," Marty said, still shouting even though he was standing directly in front of Liz now. "I don't need any advice from your family on how to raise my children. Is that clear?"

Liz didn't know what Sarah had said, but whatever it had been was clearly taken out of context. "Marty, no one is trying to tell you how to raise your children."

"No?" Marty asked. "Then why the hell is your daughter telling my kids they need to go outside? They don't want to go outside. They want their mother back,

43

and this fucking memorial isn't going to make that happen!"

Spittle flew from Marty's mouth as he shouted, and some of it landed on Liz's shirt, the rest dribbling down Marty's chin. He looked like a rabid dog that had been taken off the leash.

Liz took a moment to compose herself before she replied. The last thing she wanted to do was escalate an already volatile situation. "You are right," Liz said. "And I'm sorry for the presumptions we made in doing all this. The first thing I should've done was come to you and discussed the matter with you personally and privately. Your family's business is your own. And I never meant to step over the line. I'm sorry."

For a moment, Marty looked like he was about to calm down. But the moment passed quickly as his anger overrode any sense of rationality.

"If you, or Ben, or anyone else in your family comes near my daughters again, I promise you it will be the last time." Marty lingered, making sure the threat marinated for Liz before he turned and marched away.

Liz couldn't imagine the grief he was feeling. She had been close with Ali, and she had been a wonderful woman. She was also a fantastic mother, and the girls obviously missed her terribly.

But Liz also knew that Ali was the rock on which the foundation of the Schwartz family had been built. Marty was a good man, but he wasn't someone who could always keep things together. Ali was the binding thread of their family, and now that she was gone, the fabric of their unity was unraveling.

"Someone's not the popular girl anymore," Jane said.

Liz turned around, forgetting that Jane was still nearby. Jane was the last person Liz wanted to witness that interaction. "I was never the popular girl, Jane," Liz said.

"That's what popular girls always say," Jane said.

Her patience eroding, Liz wrapped things up with the chickens. "Just make sure they start laying eggs, or we'll have a fried chicken dinner."

"Whatever you say, boss," Jane said.

Liz flinched but then turned away. She knew Jane and the rest of the Percy family resented Ben and Liz for taking charge of the facility. But it was what the people of the community were most comfortable with, and Liz would let hell freeze over before she allowed the Percy family to control the fate of her own family.

4

*J*ane Percy had her mind working overtime after the conversation she had with Liz Riker. She had been looking for an opportunity to strike against the Riker family, and she was disappointed in herself that she hadn't seen this sooner.

For as long as Jane could remember, the Riker family had always held a high standing within the town. Ben Riker was the favored son of their community, and by association, his wife and children were held in the same high honor. But it seemed the mood was changing now that the stakes had been raised. Jane and her family were some of the few whose lot could be improved by the current landscape, and she planned to take advantage of it.

Jane returned to her portable, where her husband,

Lester, was cleaning one of their rifles. "Where's Danny?"

Lester didn't take his concentration off of his task. "He left this morning. Probably went hunting."

Jane didn't like how Danny would disappear for hours at a time, and he would always say that he was just hunting in the woods. But there had been too many days when Danny came back empty-handed. The man was too skilled of a tracker not to find at least a rabbit or squirrel.

"We need to figure out what he's really doing," Jane said.

"He told us he was hunting, so that's what he's doing," Lester said.

"You don't give your brother enough credit," Jane answered. "There's plenty of trouble still to find out there. And judging on how easily trouble finds us, I'm sure it wouldn't have taken very long to run into it."

Lester grunted something as he reassembled the weapon. Jane walked over to her bed but then paused when she noticed that her son's bed was made. He hadn't slept in their quarters for the past few nights.

"What about Gray?" Jane asked.

Lester finished assembling the weapon and then cleared the chamber before laying it down on the narrow workbench he had pulled into their portable. He was already cluttering up what limited space they had and Jane was starting to feel claustrophobic.

"I haven't seen him," Lester said.

Jane waited for more, but when her husband remained silent, she kicked the leg of their bed and raised her voice. "And who the hell have you seen?"

Lester had always been a bit of a hothead. It was one of the traits she had been attracted to. She enjoyed poking the bear and eliciting a reaction. But no matter how angry Lester became, Jane could always rein him back in. But lately, Lester had been more reserved. She wasn't sure what was going on, but it was starting to grow worrisome.

"I know you're having a hard time with him," Lester said. "I've tried talking to him, but I can't force the boy to listen to me. He's not a child anymore."

"Then he should stop acting like one," Jane said.

Lester walked over to Jane and placed large hands over her tiny shoulders. She was a very petite woman with a wiry frame, and Lester was tall and lean muscled. Together they looked like they might have been a pair of well-conditioned athletes, but based on their poor clothes, most people thought they were drug addicts.

"You're his mother," Lester answered. "And no matter how angry he gets with you, that's never going to change."

Jane wanted to remain angry, but Lester's calm demeanor was infectious. It seemed that whatever her husband was going through was causing him to mature. "You know, if I'm the only one in the relationship who gets angry now, our arguments are going to be very one-sided."

Lester grinned. The dark, black beard that had formed over his face in the past few months made his teeth look whiter. In fact, he looked better than he ever had. He had never adapted to the civilized world. He was always wild at heart, and now that the world had reverted back to days of the wild west, he was thriving.

"I don't particularly miss the fighting," Lester said. "But I do miss the making up."

Lester kissed her, and she felt his hands wandering down her backside. She kissed him back harder, biting down on his lower lip.

After they had lain on the cot, and after making love, Jane's head was much clearer. They dressed when they were finished and then sat side by side on the edge of the cot.

"They're falling apart out there," Jane said.

Lester lay back down and closed his eyes. "The whole world is falling apart. I don't know what made you think this place was going to be any different."

Jane shook her head. "I mean Liz. She's stretched too thin, and with Ben gone, everything has fallen on her shoulders."

"Yeah, well, Ben will come back," Lester said. "He's annoying that way."

Jane turned around and faced her husband. "I think we might be able to take control of this place."

Lester opened his eyes. "If we make a move against

this place, then the Rikers make a move against us, and we're right back to where we started."

"I'm not talking about starting a fight," Jane said. "I'm talking about winning over the people here at the facility."

Lester scoffed and shut his eyes again. "I think you have a better chance of us flying to the moon than that happening."

Jane slapped Lester's arm. "I'm serious. People are on edge. And after the debacle with Marty's wife, people are starting to lose faith. And there is that other woman, the one who lost her husband that first day. She blames Ben for her husband's death. And it's not like the Rikers have been completely steadfast in everything they've done. They have chinks in their armor. We can expose that and use it against them."

Lester opened one eye. "So, you think those chickens are going to win everybody over?"

"I think it's a start," Jane answered. "But we have to do more than just prove to people that we can lead them. We also need to chip away at the Rikers reputation."

Lester drummed his fingers over his flat stomach, giving it some thought. "If we try to sabotage anything, the Rikers are just going to blame us. And our reputation is just as notorious as theirs. It's a steep hill to climb, Jane."

"What did I tell you when all this started?" Jane asked. "This is a new beginning for anybody strong enough to take advantage of it. We can do this if we commit to it. All of us. You, me, Danny, and Gray."

Lester reached for Jane's hand. "Then I think the first step is you and Gray figuring things out."

"I've tried," Jane said. "The boy's as stubborn as I am."

"He is," Lester said. "He's like you in a lot of ways." His voice grew softer. "Part of me has always been glad about that."

Jane pulled her husband's face toward hers and looked him in the eye. "And I've always hated that he hasn't been more like you. He might be smart, but he doesn't have your grit."

Jane leaned in for another kiss when their door opened, and Gray stepped inside. The moment Gray saw his parents in bed, even though they were fully clothed, he looked away.

"Oh, sorry," Gray said.

"Don't be such a prude," Jane said, sliding off the bed. "Where have you been?"

Gray looked at his mother with the same contempt he had worn ever since he learned the truth about what she had done while he was unconscious. "I've been out."

Jane wasn't going to take the cold shoulder any longer. She marched over to him and forced him to look her in the eye. "Don't give me that horseshit. You may not agree with what I did, but you're still my

JAMES HUNT

responsibility. And right now, I don't need you walking around causing trouble for us."

Gray removed his arm out of his mother's grasp. "I'm not causing trouble."

Lester got out of bed, and Gray took one step back. The last time the father and son had confronted one another, Lester had slapped Gray across the face. The blow had nearly ripped the stitches in his neck that had kept him alive after his gunshot wound.

"Your mother needs to talk to you," Lester said. "I suggest you listen."

"Fine," Gray said. "I'm listening."

Gray might have just been staying to appease her, but Jane wasn't going to waste it.

"You should understand that what I did to Nancy's mother was an act of mercy," Jane said.

Gray scoffed and shook his head, muttering something beneath his breath.

"She was a woman who had lost her way and was in incredible pain," Jane said. "She was going to kill us, and you, even Nancy."

Gray raised his eyebrows. "Is that it?"

Jane was at her wit's end. She didn't know how else to reach her son and convince him that what she did might've been violent, but it was necessary. She desperately wanted him to forgive her even though she didn't believe she had anything to be forgiven for. To not have the trust of her son was slowly eating away at her soul.

Jane grabbed Gray's hands and held them in hers.

She gripped them tightly. "No matter how angry you are with me or what you think of me, I will always be your mother. And I will always do what I think is necessary to keep you safe. No matter the cost." She let go of his hands and stepped back.

Jane studied her son's reaction and saw that he had softened from her words despite his effort to remain angry. He cleared his throat and then grabbed a fresh pair of clothes off the bed.

"Okay," Gray said.

Jane watched as Gray left, shutting the door behind him. Lester walked up behind her and grabbed her waistline.

"Well," Jane said. "I guess that's a start."

"He'll warm up," Lester said. "He loves you too much even though he's too stubborn to admit it right now."

Jane appreciated her husband's thoughtful words, but she wasn't sure how much love her son had left to show. She had sensed him separating from the family for years, and maybe this was the final act that broke his link to his family. But what broke her heart the most was the fact that Gray believed his family was playing the role of the evil villain. But in life, there were very few things that were black and white. She only hoped that Gray realized that before it was too late to salvage his relationship with his family.

5

*N*ancy Simmons picked up another empty ration crate from the trash and then walked over to the field's open space beyond the fence line of the fire facility. In her right arm, she kept the rifle cradled, and then she stood in the well-worn spot of grass where she had been coming every day for the past three weeks for target practice.

It had been a beautiful morning, with clear blue skies, though it was growing warmer, and Nancy's shirt was stained with sweat around the neck, pits, and back. She adjusted her grip on both the old carton and the rifle.

Nancy aimed for a point in the sky and concentrated on the fixed position. She took a few deep breaths to keep her heart rate steady and then flung the carton high into the air. As the piece of trash arched against the blue sky, Nancy raised her rifle to track it.

She only had a few seconds to aim before the target plummeted to the ground. She adjusted her stance, placed her finger on the trigger, exhaled, and then fired.

The bullet connected with the carton and flung it forward a little bit before it landed in a larger pile of trash with the dozens of other targets she had hit that morning.

Nancy lowered the rifle, smoke wafting from the end of the rifle. "Twenty-three."

It was a new record of consecutive shots since she had started practicing with the weapon. She remembered when she couldn't even hit a target standing still, and now she was flinging targets into the air by herself and hitting bullseyes.

The hours of endless training of both her mind and her body were starting to pay off. She felt stronger, her body more toned and athletic, and she was able to see things more clearly than ever before. It was amazing what she could do when she no longer cared about what type of makeup she was wearing, or the designer clothes that all the other girls thought were popular.

Looking back at all that now made her feel silly about ever enjoying those things. Cheerleading, boys, clothes, social status, they were all meaningless now. But that was a different time and a different life. The world no longer valued pretty things, and Nancy couldn't rely on her looks anymore. All that mattered now was what you brought to the table for survival.

And Nancy was tired of taking a backseat, so she decided to do something about it.

Nancy pocketed the rest of her ammunition and gathered up all of the empty boxes with bullet holes in them, and once she had bagged everything, she flung the black trash bag over her shoulder, the black plastic hot from the late-morning sun, and headed toward the compound.

On the way back toward the front gate, Nancy passed the graveyards set up outside the fence's perimeter. There were several crosses marked over mounds of dirt. They had lost quite a few people since all this had started, but most folks still had at least some of their family intact.

Nancy was one of the exceptions. The moment of the EMP's detonation, her entire life had changed. In the course of a few milliseconds, the trajectory of her future had completely shifted course. But a part of her was glad to have a new lease on life. She had an opportunity that few people ever had the chance to receive: a fresh start.

Nancy could completely rebuild her image and how she wanted people to see her. She no longer wanted to be seen as the lazy, pretty girl. She wanted to be known as a survivor, someone formidable who could hold her own. And she believed she was finally turning a corner of becoming that version of herself.

Once she returned to the facility, Nancy passed the cluster of tents in the open field by the front gates where the women from the clinic she and Sarah had brought back had set up camp. It had been Sarah's decision to bring the women back with them, despite Nancy's protest. She knew bringing more people would make it difficult for their already dwindling resources.

So far, between rationing and hunting, everyone had remained fed. Nancy had gone out a few times with the hunting party. As her shooting improved, so did the number of critters she managed to bag and bring back. The other guys she hunted with still complained that she was too loud.

"I heard you out there, Gunslinger."

Nancy didn't bother turning around. She knew it was Willie. "You should come out with me sometime," Nancy said. "I could always use a target with legs."

Willie laughed and appeared on her left, smoking a cigarette. He was a tall man and had a bad-boy image about him. He was also in his late twenties and was a woman beater. She and Sarah had found him holding a baseball bat above his girlfriend's head at the clinic, where they had found the other women, ready to beat the life out of her.

Nancy was convinced he would've done it if they hadn't shown up. But Willie's girlfriend, Carolina, who had been the subject of his abuse, had begged Nancy and Sarah not to hurt him. And because he hadn't actually hit anyone in front of them, Sarah told Nancy it wasn't their place to cut in.

"You know if you keep flirting with me like that, Carolina will get jealous," Willie said.

Nancy tensed, and it took all of her restraint not to swing her rifle at his head.

"Maybe you could show me how to use that someday?" Willie asked.

Nancy finally stopped walking and dropped the bag of trash next to her leg. She kept her rifle at the ready, her finger on the trigger.

Willie tilted his head to the side in a playful way. "Did I say something wrong, Gunslinger?"

"I know you think nobody's watching anymore," Nancy said. "But I haven't taken my eyes off of you."

Willie stepped closer. "That makes two of us."

Nancy nudged the end of her rifle against Willy's stomach, but the gesture which she had hoped would make him back off only made him press against the weapon even harder.

"You're going to slip up," Nancy said. "And when you do, I'll be there to bring you down."

Willie concentrated on her with a predator's gaze. Nancy didn't have much experience with men like Willie growing up. Her father had been a kind man, and all of the boys she had thought she was interested in at school were simply that, boys. But Willie was a dangerous man. A man who was not afraid to cross boundaries.

"You know you talk a big game, but there's a difference between shooting trash and killing another person," Willie said. "Is that something you think you can do?"

"What makes you think I haven't done that already?" Nancy asked.

Willie smiled and shook his head. "You might have killed somebody out of necessity, but you've never killed anyone out of anger."

Nancy hated the fact that Willie was so perceptive when it came to reading people. She supposed that was a skill he learned in order to identify women he could take advantage of. But Nancy wasn't the same weak schoolgirl who had arrived at the facility.

"No better time to learn than the present," Nancy said.

The pair remained in a standoff until Willie eventually smiled again and laughed as he stepped back, putting a few feet between himself and the end of Nancy's rifle.

"Then I guess I should get out of your way before you put a slug in my belly," Willie said.

Willie turned away, lighting another cigarette and chuckling to himself. He was muttering something beneath his breath, but Nancy couldn't hear what he said. She watched him until he vanished into his tent and then lingered to make sure he stayed inside. She knew it was a mistake having him here, but because he hadn't shown any real aggression toward anyone since he had arrived, Mr. and Mrs. Riker had decided to keep him close to at least keep an eye on him.

Nancy picked up the bag of trash and carried it around to the dumpster on the backside of the main building. She lingered there for a moment, looking at the back door.

Willie wasn't the only man Nancy had been keeping a close eye on. It was tempting to go inside, but she knew continuing their conversation would only draw attention from the rest of the community. She still wasn't sure how she felt about him, but she was certain that Mr. and Mrs. Riker would not approve of the thoughts circling her head.

It was curiosity initially, but the more Nancy spoke with him, the more she wanted to know. He wasn't what she had expected him to be, and while Abe had done some terrible things, he at least wanted to redeem himself.

Unable to stay away, Nancy shouldered the rifle and opened the door. The back entrance of the mess hall led into a closet, and she fumbled her way forward in the darkness until she found the door that led into the kitchen.

It was well past breakfast, so the mess hall and the kitchen were empty, but it would be bustling with activity in about two hours as everybody returned for lunch.

In many ways, living at the facility was kind of like being at school. There was a regimented schedule that everybody adhered to. Everybody ate breakfast, lunch, and dinner together. Between meals, there was work to be done, but the biggest difference between school and the facility was the fact that if Nancy screwed up, it could come at the cost of someone's life.

Nancy stepped through the kitchen and headed toward the storage locker and found the one that had been converted to a holding cell.

There was no guard, and the door was open, but the man inside was tethered by a chain around his ankle that gave him enough room to walk around the space but not to escape. But he hadn't tried to escape since he was brought here, and Nancy wondered when Mr. and Mrs. Riker were going to let him roam free.

Abe looked up from the book he'd been reading on his cot, which was pushed up against the wall where his chains were tethered. He smiled when he saw her and set the book aside. "What are you doing here?"

"I was out practicing shooting some of the discarded MRE packaging," Nancy answered. "I was on my way back in when I decided to stop by and see how you're doing." She gestured to the book. "I didn't know you liked to read."

Abe glanced at the cover of the novel. It was an old Stephen King book, Pet Cemetery. "I didn't think my current situation was frightening enough, so I thought I'd raise the stakes."

"Anything else you've been up to?" Nancy asked.

Abe folded his hands in his lap and gestured around to the very drab surroundings. "Just getting a little R&R." He grinned, and it was a kind of easy-going smile she remembered seeing on movie stars. But this man was no actor.

"Well, is there anything I can ask the hotel manager to do to help make your stay more comfortable?" Nancy asked, playing along.

Abe rubbed his chin and furrowed his brow, giving it considerable thought before he answered. "I think I'll take my lunch in my room today. I'll have a filet mignon, mashed potatoes, and asparagus."

Nancy nodded. "Excellent choice, sir. Would you care for any dessert?"

"What would you recommend?" Abe asked.

"The hummingbird cake is delicious," Nancy answered.

"Then I'll take two slices," Abe replied.

Nancy crossed her arms beneath her chest. "And who is the second slice for?"

"Oh, they're both for me," Abe answered. "After all, I'm on vacation."

"And what a vacation it is," Nancy said.

Abe dropped some of the playfulness, and he swung his legs off the side of the cot. He was tall and lean, with a very thick beard covering his face. It made him look much older, though he was only twenty. He looked like a homeless man in his current state, but there were a lot of people who look like that these days. But it was his eyes that betrayed his hard stare; there was genuine kindness in him.

"I didn't think the warden wanted you to swing by here anymore," Abe said.

"Yeah, well, the warden isn't around today," Nancy said. "So I decided to make up my own visitation hours."

The chain around Abe's ankle only allowed him to get within a few feet of her. And Nancy remained in the doorway, never entering the cooler. It was an invisible barrier that she had constructed between them because, despite her curiosity of him and his seemingly good-natured smile, he had made choices that helped kill innocent people, even though he never pulled the trigger himself.

Abe was part of an organization called The New Order, and they had been responsible for the EMP that detonated and destroyed their modern way of life. No more lights, no more phones or computers, no cars or any type of transportation—nothing electronic. Their way of life had been completely flipped upside down, and there was nothing they could do to change that fact. All that was left now was to pick up the pieces.

"Yeah, well, I don't think this is a hotel I'll ever check out of," Abe said.

"Did you talk to Mr. Riker?" Nancy asked.

Abe nodded. "But that doesn't forgive me for what I've done."

"It wasn't all your fault," Nancy said. "They brainwashed you."

Abe avoided eye contact with her. "I brainwashed myself."

"They were using you," Nancy said. "I know you aren't a bad person. But none of that matters if you don't see yourself in the same way."

Nancy wasn't sure if any of what she was saying was penetrating that thick wall of propaganda those people had drilled into his head. She hoped that one day it would finally click for him, but she could tell by the look in his eyes that it wasn't today.

"I don't know, Nancy," Abe said. "I just don't know."

Every time Abe spoke this way, it made Nancy recoil. This wasn't the same person she had built up in her head, but the conversations were a reality check, one that she needed.

Nancy turned to leave, adjusting the rifle on her shoulder when she Abe called out to her. She spun around.

"Maybe I've missed my chance," Abe said. "Maybe it is too late for me."

"It's never too late," Nancy said. "I've adapted to this world, Abe. You can, too."

Nancy could tell he wanted to say something more, but he held his tongue. Whatever he was thinking about, he kept to himself. It was difficult and frustrating, but she had to treat this just like she did with everything else in this new world. It would take patience, time, and a relentless effort before she saw any improvement.

The way forward was never easy, and no one knew that better than Nancy. She left Abe to his sulking, and when she stepped back outside, she saw Mr. Riker trotting toward the front entrance with another man in tow. She looked up at the tower and saw their marksman keeping a bead on them all the way up until Mr. Riker gave the signal to the shooter in the tower to stand down.

But Nancy didn't relax as she walked over to where Mr. Riker tied off the horses.

"Mr. Riker," Nancy said. "How did it go?"

Mr. Riker quickly tied off the lead to the horse and then planted a bucket of grain in front of the animals. "They didn't kill me. Do me a favor and brush the horses down, okay?"

"Yeah, sure," Nancy answered.

Mr. Riker didn't even look her in the eye as he walked over to the man he'd brought back. He was dressed in military fatigues, and Nancy assumed this was another soldier from the military base that Mr. Riker had struck up an alliance with. There had been another man who had come back with him the first time, but he had been killed by one of the enemy terrorists along with some of their own.

But as Nancy watched Mr. Riker escort the military man into the main building, Nancy hoped Mr. Riker wasn't planning on doing anything rash with Abe.

It would be a shame to lose another good man.

6

———

The entire ride from the military installation all the way back to the fire facility, Ben was thinking about what happened next. He knew Jackson wanted confirmation of the information he'd given him, but he wasn't sure if hearing it from Abe would be enough.

"How long has the prisoner been here?" Jackson asked, walking with Ben toward the main building where he was kept.

"Since the second day after the EMP strike," Ben answered. "We don't keep a guard on him anymore, but we still keep him chained in one of the storage coolers. He hasn't given us any problems since he's been here."

"If I knew any better, I would say that you had a soft spot for the guy," Jackson said.

"Maybe I do," Ben said. "That first day of the attack, I was caught off guard by one of the enemy soldiers in the woods coming out of Asheville. I had my two boys with me, and Abe could have killed all three of us. He had the drop on me, but he chose to let us go. The man isn't a killer."

"He's still a part of the enemy," Jackson said. "And he should be treated accordingly."

Ben stepped in front of Jackson, blocking his path. "You may not agree with everything I've done, but the only reason you're still alive is because of the warning I gave you before the attack on your facility. I didn't have to risk my neck to tell you about the enemy that was coming. But I did."

"You also did it because you wanted help," Jackson said. "So, don't take the high road and pretend you're better than I am. We both want something here. I suggest we work together in order to make sure the enemy doesn't blow us all off the face of the earth."

"And I suggest you let me take the lead on this," Ben said. "Because you're not the commander of this facility. Understand?"

Ben wasn't sure if the strong show of force would make Jackson understand who was in charge. But it seemed the commander respected somebody who could put their foot down, and Jackson simply nodded, setting his mouth in a coy smile.

It was still a few hours until lunch, so the building was empty save for their lonc prisoner. Ben walked over to the cooler where Abe was being held and found him taking a nap.

"Time to get up," Ben said.

Abe kept his eyes closed with his hands folded over his stomach. "I was hoping today might be a good day." He opened his eyes and propped himself up onto his elbows, staring at Ben and Jackson. "I can see now that was simply a dream."

Ben entered the storage room, and Jackson followed suit. "This is Lieutenant Colonel Jackson. He was operating a military installation nearby that was attacked by The New Order."

"And?" Abe asked.

Ben stepped forward, hands on his hips as he stared down. "And we need to know what else they're planning, including as much detail on their nuclear weapon program that you can tell us. We want to be one step ahead of them while we can."

Ben wasn't sure how Abe would react to this encounter, but he hoped the man wouldn't say or do anything to provoke Jackson. He didn't strike Ben as the kind of guy who would lash out for no reason so long as Jackson remained civilized, so would Abe.

"It sounds like you're doing just fine without me," Abe said, and he started to close his eyes again.

Ben quickly moved to Abe's cot and ripped out the man's pillow from beneath his head. He flung it to the floor, lowering his voice. "You need to help me, so I can help you," Ben said. "Because the man behind me isn't in the mood to play nice, and my family is in danger the longer we stay here. You once told me that you wanted penance for what you've done. Well, this is the first step."

Ben released Abe and then stepped back. The man remained on the cot rubbing his arm where Ben had grabbed him.

"Well?" Ben asked.

"I already told you what I know," Abe said.

"So tell me," Jackson replied. "Or does it bother you that we killed some of your friends?"

Ben jumped in and started talking before Abe could retaliate. "If your people come back, they are going to return in a much larger force. The only way this facility stays safe is if we have the military backing us up, and in order for that to happen, you need to tell Jackson about the bomb."

"This is a waste of time," Jackson said. "You give me fifteen minutes alone with him and I'll have all the information we need."

"I won't break as easily as you think," Abe said.

"Yeah, well, we will see about that," Jackson said.

"Hey," Ben said, catching Abe's attention, "we're out of options. And your life is not more valuable than my family's life."

Abe grimaced and then shuffled his feet before staring down at his toes. He muttered something beneath his breath and then drew in a long, slow breath. "Your best chance at stopping the bomb is finding a weapons camp."

"What's that?" Ben asked.

"Places where civilians would make things for the cause," Abe answered. "I remember them talking about them right before the EMP went off. The New Order doesn't have enough fighters on their side, so they thought getting modern weaponry back up and running was the best way to keep the fight competitive against you guys." He gestured to Jackson.

"And what exactly are they building at these camps?" Jackson asked.

"I told you I don't know the specifics," Abe answered. "All I know is that the weapons are supposed to give The New Order an edge against the military."

"And do you have a location for these camps?" Ben asked.

"I know of one," Abe answered. "It was where I was supposed to rendezvous with my unit after I blew the dam outside of Asheville. It's in a small town south of here. I'm trying to remember the name. I think it started with an E."

"Eustis?" Ben asked.

"Yeah," Abe answered. "Yeah, that was the name of it. That's where one of the work camps should be stationed. If you want to know more about the nuke they're building, then that's where you should start."

Ben turned to Jackson and lowered his voice so Abe couldn't hear. "If we get to Eustis and can confirm what they're doing, we might be able to stop them."

Jackson kept his attention on Abe, and Ben feared

that the colonel was growing agitated with the lack of information.

"How many fighting men are supposed to be stationed at this camp?" Jackson asked. "Or is that too specific a question?"

"They are smaller camps," Abe answered. "Not like what you saw outside of Charlotte, Ben."

"So it's probably less than a few dozen?" Ben asked.

Abe nodded. "And if they have managed to re-create some of the more heavy-duty weapons, then it could be more than enough to hold back forces with inferior firepower."

"Anything else?" Ben asked.

"The people in charge of The New Order are ruthless," Abe said. "I suppose that's something you guys know by now, considering everything that you've seen. But they have a conviction, and everyone in their organization from the very top to the very bottom believes in their mission."

"And what exactly is that mission?" Jackson asked.

"Destroy everything and make sure it never works again."

"Well," Ben said, "I guess we better get moving."

Ben led Jackson out of the building, and once they were out of earshot from Abe, Jackson had a few choice words for Ben.

"You're on a first-name basis with your prisoner?" Jackson asked. "You don't have much experience in all of this, do you?"

"Look, I know you have your preconceived notions about that guy based off of the organization he's with," Ben answered. "And no, I don't have a lot of experience with this kind of thing. Up until the EMP went off, I was a Lieutenant with the Asheville Fire Department. But I just handed you some very valuable intelligence about an enemy that poses a threat to everyone. So why don't you drop the attitude so we can get this done?"

Jackson looked like he was about to deck Ben, but thankfully, it didn't come to blows. "How far is it from here to Eustis?" Jackson asked.

"At least a three-hour horseback ride," Ben answered. "But I only have two horses. That's not enough to carry any of your men."

"I'm not taking any of my men," Jackson said. "It's just going to be you and me."

Ben frowned. "Did you hear what he was saying? They're making weapons so they can gain an edge against the military. You and I are hardly an army."

"I'm still not convinced that guy is telling the truth," Jackson said. "That's why you and I are going to investigate this intelligence ourselves and see if it's worth bringing in support to handle it."

"Why would he lie?" Ben asked.

"I don't know," Jackson answered. "Why would he join an organization and then turn his back on them? As far as I'm concerned, this guy's loyalty can be bought. He would say anything to make sure that we didn't pry off his fingernails. So that's why you and I are going to go investigate this intelligence and determine if he is telling the truth. That's the deal, Ben. You want my help to save your little community here? Then you help me uncover something tangible that I can bring back to my commanders. Is that understood?"

Ben knew he was stuck between a rock and a hard place. He needed Jackson's support when it came to obtaining any military intervention for his people.

"Okay," Ben answered. "But if we do find something there, if Abe was telling the truth, everybody here at this facility is protected by the military. You guys fight for this place like it was your home base. Deal?"

"Deal. Now, you go and get what you need to in order for us to make a stand against this camp," Jackson said. "And make sure you pack one for me, too." He clapped Ben on the shoulder and then started to walk away.

"And where are you going?" Ben asked.

"Take a look around," Jackson answered. "I'd ask for a tour, but I know you're busy."

Ben watched as Jackson cruised around the facility. He didn't like the idea of the colonel walking around unsupervised, and when he saw Nancy nearby, he pulled her closer.

"I want you to keep an eye on him," Ben said.

"He's the colonel?" Nancy asked.

"Yeah," Ben answered. "I don't think he's going to

cause any trouble, but just make sure nobody messes with him while he's looking around, okay?"

Nancy nodded. She had come a long way since the EMP was detonated. She was almost unrecognizable, and Ben knew she had gone through a lot of suffering to get to this point.

"Thank you," Ben said. "And watch your back."

"Will do, Mr. Riker," Nancy said.

Nancy followed Jackson, and Ben headed toward their portable so he could speak with Liz. He needed to catch her up to speed on what was going on so she could handle the affairs here at the facility while he was gone. But as he finished telling Liz about the plan, she didn't react the way he thought she would.

"I don't want you to go," Liz said.

"It's not like I am excited to go myself," Ben replied. "That's the deal Jackson wanted to make."

"Then make a new deal," Liz replied. "How much more do we have to give this guy before we lose everything."

Ben knew she was stressed. Ever since Sarah had been taken by Mark, she had been on edge. But that was the reason why Ben knew he needed to go. "We don't have the manpower to withstand a full assault from the enemy."

"But you don't know if they'll even find us," Liz said. "You're basing all of this on a hunch."

"Mark knows where we are," Ben said. "It's only a matter of time before he tells his people about us."

"How can you be sure Mark will tell his people about us?" Liz asked. "I know the two of you have a terrible history with one another, but he had an opportunity to kill you and Sarah, but he didn't do it. Don't you think that means something?"

"It means he has another chance," Ben answered. "I need to go and make this right so we don't have trouble in the long term. Okay?"

It was clear Liz didn't agree with his argument, but she dropped the subject and helped him pack to leave for the trip. Once they had enough rations for Ben and Jackson, along with a few emergency supplies should they get held up, Ben kissed and hugged his boys.

"Do you really have to leave again?" Tommy asked.

Tommy was the youngest, and he puffed out his lower lip to signal that he really didn't want Ben to go. But his older brother Connor put his arm around his brother's shoulder.

"It's okay, Tommy," Connor said. "Dad's going because he has to keep us safe. Right, Dad?"

Both boys looked up at him, and Ben felt his heart melt. "That's right. And I need you two to help keep your mom and sister safe while I'm gone. Can you do that for me?"

Connor nodded, but Tommy kept his head down.

Ben crouched and tilted his youngest boy's chin up so he could look Tommy in the eye. "I know it's hard, son," Ben said. "But I need you to be brave for me, all right?"

"I don't want to be brave," Tommy answered. "I just want you to stay here."

As hard as all of this had been for Ben and the rest of the adults, it was even more difficult for the children. Their lives had been completely turned upside down. Liz walked up behind both boys and placed her hands on top of their heads. Tommy wrapped his arms around his mother and held on tight. Ben stood and kissed Liz before turning around and joining Jackson by the horses.

"That's a fine-looking family you have," Jackson said.

"Thanks," Ben said.

"I understand your trepidation," Jackson said. "I really do. But you have to understand that I don't have a lot of resources at my disposal. If this turns out to be nothing—and for the record, I hope that's not the case —I would have wasted precious time that my men could have been using to prepare to evacuate the facility we were charged with guarding. I know you think that's not a big deal, but it's my duty. And I take that duty seriously."

Ben hadn't considered the risk Jackson was taking in trusting him. Despite everything that had happened, Jackson was still fused to the chain of command.

"Mr. Riker?"

Ben turned around, surprised to find Gray Percy standing behind him. "Gray, what are you doing out here?"

"I was hoping to catch you before you left," Gray said. The scars on his neck were still visible from where Ben had stitched him up after he'd been shot. "I haven't had an opportunity to thank you for what you did."

"I'm glad I was there to help," Ben said.

Gray stood there awkwardly for a moment, and Ben couldn't help but see his mother in him. They shared the same wiry frame, though Gray inherited his father's height. "If there's anything I can do to help out around here, I just want you to know that I'm ready. I feel a lot better, and I've got my strength back, so I'm ready to go."

Ben nodded. "That's good to hear. Why don't you speak with Mrs. Riker, and she'll set you up with something?"

Gray smiled. "Sounds good." He turned to leave, and Ben had the sudden urge to reach out to him one last time.

"Gray," Ben said, causing the boy to turn around. "How are your folks?"

Gray's smile vanished. "Unfortunately, the same." He turned around and disappeared.

"That kid looked kind of depressed for having a second lease on life," Jackson said.

Ben mounted his horse and then looked back to Gray before turning to Jackson. "He's had a rough go of it. Comes from a hard family."

"Family can make or break a man," Jackson said.

Ben offered one final glance at his own family, Jackson's words radiating through his head. "Yes, they can."

Ben and Jackson headed for the gate, Ben glancing behind him one last time at the facility. Because while it looked nothing like the house he had built with Liz when they were first married, it was still home.

Every single person Ben cared about lived here now. His sons, his wife, and his surviving friends. He was doing his best to keep everyone alive, but if he couldn't convince Jackson to give him the reinforcements he needed to keep them safe, Ben wasn't sure how much longer they would survive.

7

The town's sign had been graffitied over, but Mark could still see the original name underneath. Casselberry was one of the smaller mountain towns in the area, with a population of less than one thousand. But it was on the quickest path on their journey toward Asheville, and Mark had no time to waste to go around it.

The fight ahead of them in Asheville would be the first real test of their strength since the EMP was detonated. And while Mark was confident in his own abilities, he wasn't sure about the rest of his unit.

Mark led a force of one hundred men. He had wanted more, but the supreme leader instructed him that one hundred men were more than enough to go up against any battalion. He liked to reference the Spartans against the Persians and how only one hundred Spartans repelled an entire army, fighting all the way down to the last man.

It wasn't that Mark was afraid to die, but ever since Mark had run into his brother back in their home-town, there had been a cloud of doubt circling over-head. He couldn't get his brother's voice out of his brain. Ben was like Jiminy Cricket preaching against the evil in Mark's heart.

Mark had never been conflicted in his mission, but a crack had appeared in the once invincible armor that was his loyalty.

"Sir," one of the scouts appeared from the woods on the side of the road. "The town is half a mile down the road around the bend. They have two sentries stationed on either side of the town on the main road access points, but there is no other security through the woods."

"If they have the brains to post sentries, then they at least know how to defend themselves," Mark said. "Did you get a count of how many fighters they have?"

The scout nodded. "I counted at least three dozen armed men walking the streets, maybe the same amount tucked away in the houses and stores. It's a smaller community, and while the other places we've encountered have had weapons, I don't expect this to be any different. These are fighters, sir, like us."

"No," Mark said. "Not like us at all. Have the number two and three teams on standby in the woods. Everyone else follows me to the front."

"Yes, sir." The scout dispersed to deliver the commands.

Normally, Mark didn't need to pep talk himself when it came to his missions. He had always been able to turn it on when he needed to and then turn it off when he was finished. But for the entirety of that last half mile, Mark couldn't get his head on straight.

As Mark neared the front of the town with his men, he saw the two guards the scout told him would be waiting for them. They were both middle-aged men armed with hunting rifles.

"I think that's far enough," the first guard said.

Mark held up his hand, and his men slowed to a stop behind him. They had marched on foot, and to the small towns they had come across, they looked like a ragtag group of men searching for shelter or food. But they were far more dangerous.

"What brings you to our neck of the woods?" The sentry who spoke was a heavyset man wearing a dirtied white crew shirt and jeans.

"We come with good news," Mark said, "for anyone willing to listen."

The pair of sentries exchanged a glance, and then the heavyset one spoke again. "And what good news would that be?"

"Yeah, did you bring the power with you?" the second sentry asked and then chuckled to himself. He had a high-pitched laugh, but it matched his small frame. The man couldn't have weighed more than one-twenty soaking wet. The rifle in his hands was almost as big as he was.

"No power," Mark said. "Just an opportunity."

Mark noted the number of people slowly gathering at the front of the town now. It seemed their curiosity outweighed their fear. From the looks of them, Mark didn't think these folks had suffered much. Casselberry was so far away from any major city that they had probably escaped the wrath from their main units after the EMP was detonated. These people might not even know what was going on.

"And what opportunity is that?" the heavyset sentry asked, keeping his rifle at the ready despite no sign of aggression from Mark and his people. Not that it would make a difference.

"To join a cause," Mark said, taking a few steps forward and now speaking more to the people who had come forth from the town to see what was going on. "There is a movement happening in this country, and all of you have seen the effects of it. We're here to find out who has the will and determination to see this cause through to the end."

As with most of the towns Mark visited, everybody who listened to him looked confused. And while some murmurs were coming from the crowd gathering behind the two sentries, it was the heavyset guard with his rifle still up and aimed at no one in particular who spoke up.

"You trying to tell me that you people are the ones who caused all of this?" the sentry asked.

It was rare for Mark to come across somebody who put two and two together so quickly. And he noticed that the fat man's question sparked worry in the townspeople.

"We are the ones who took the first steps," Mark said. "We are the ones who were strong enough to take hold of an opportunity. All we want for the people in this country is a new start."

"My mother died because of you assholes," a voice shouted from the back. "She couldn't get her insulin because all the refrigerators were turned off."

The crowd started to turn against Mark and his men, and he noticed that a few more townspeople with weapons made their way toward the front.

"We are The New Order," Mark shouted, realizing that these people would choose the hard path. "And we are here to bring you the only opportunity you'll ever need." He flashed the patch on his shoulder so people could see. "Join our movement, and you will be given priority in the new world we build together."

"And if we refuse?" the heavyset guard asked.

Mark sighed, and again he heard his brother's voice echo in the back of his mind. "Then we will kill you and take what resources you have in the town in the name of our cause. The choice is yours."

It was quiet for a moment after that, as it usually was. People never believed it was the end, even when you told them it was coming. Mark had always blamed humanity's eternal optimism. It seemed that no matter what we faced as a species, we always believed that we could overcome the impossible.

But there would be no impossible feats today.

"From what I can see, we have you outnumbered," the heavyset man said, and to his credit, he didn't sound scared, but the skinny sentry stationed next to him was shaking enough for the both of them. "So why don't you turn your merry little band of men around and get out of here before we do some damage to your 'new order.'"

All Mark had to do was give the signal and the two units stationed on either side of the town would attack, killing more people in the first few minutes than was necessary to bring the conflict to a swift and abrupt end. It was how it always went every time they took a town. They had never come up against an adversary that they couldn't defeat, and Mark knew this place would be no different.

"Is there no one who will stand with us?" Mark asked.

Most people just stared blankly ahead, everyone too scared to think for themselves, but he saw a few people defiantly shake their heads. He respected those individuals. At least they knew what they wanted and were brave enough to make their stand. He hoped that made a difference when they died.

Mark raised his hand, and in the two seconds that

followed, the town's armed gunmen were dropping like flies as gunfire erupted from the woods.

Because the gunfire was coming from all directions, the townspeople scattered in random directions. Their aimless retreat provided ample opportunities for Mark's men to shoot and kill.

Because of the distraction from both sides of the town, the sentries were overwhelmed as Mark advanced. The heavyset man only fired once before he took a bullet to the head. The skinny one dropped his weapon and held up his hands in the air, but one of Mark's fighters stuck a knife in the skinny man's belly and gutted him in the street.

But Mark did not engage in any fighting. He normally would have been in the mix with the rest of his men, but he remained frozen in the same spot from where he had given his initial signal to attack. The violence that he witnessed seemed more gruesome as he watched from the outside.

There was something euphoric about fighting whenever you were in the middle of it. There really wasn't anything like killing a man, watching the life drain from him. And all the times that Mark had fought in these skirmishes with his men, he now wondered if he had the same smile that so many of his men were wearing as they fought and killed.

After less than ten minutes, anybody who wasn't dead had already thrown down their weapons and surrendered. The scout who had reported to Mark about the town returned with a bloodstained uniform.

"The town is secure, sir," the scout said.

Mark nodded and then followed the scout into the streets, passing the motionless bodies on the pavement. The town was silent now save for the crying, which always sounded much louder after the gunfire had subsided.

"Those men lined up on their knees are what's left of their leadership group," the scout said. "They said they are willing to make a deal now." The scout laughed, and Mark nodded in response. "We kept them alive just so you could string them along."

Mark winced. He had developed a reputation for being ruthless in his interrogations of survivors. He had gotten so good at it and done it for so long that he couldn't remember a time before he did such terrible things. He was unsure of when he had crossed that line, but it was buried beneath all of the dead bodies he had left behind in his wake.

Mark approached the first man on his knees who had his head down. He wasn't shaking or crying. He just looked tired.

"I was told you now wanted to negotiate," Mark said.

The man lifted his head, and he sported a gash along his forehead that caused blood to drip down his face. Because his hands were tied behind his back, he couldn't wipe the blood from his eyes, so he kept them shut.

"Take what supplies you want," the bloodied man said. "Just don't kill anybody else. We've already lost too many."

Mark stared down at the man for a long moment, and he wondered just how many loved ones and friends had been killed since all this started. How many children were now orphaned? How many spouses without their significant others? How many friends dead?

"I gave you and your people a chance," Mark said. "This is the fate that you chose for yourselves."

The man struggled to open his eyes. "You came at us with an ultimatum of servitude or death. What kind of choices are those? You speak like a liberator but act as a dictator."

"I don't need a lecture from you," Mark said, growing agitated. "Life doesn't take kindly to the weak. You're the one who couldn't push us back."

The bloodied man bowed his head. His shoulder started to tremble, and at first, Mark believed that the man was crying. When he lifted his head again, Mark retreated a step when he saw the man was smiling.

"You hear the sound of your crusade?" The bloodied man turned his head to the side and leaned forward slightly. "Listen."

It grew quiet again, and Mark heard the sobs of the

townspeople. Parents comforted children, friends whispered encouragement, and loved ones spoke of how much they cared for one another. Amidst so much fear and pain, there was still hope. Hope that they might somehow survive and see one more sunrise. It was the condition of the human spirit to always keep fighting. To find something to cling to and hold on to for dear life so that you might survive the darkness that comes for everyone.

"That's the sound of your liberation," the bloodied man said. "People fear what you will do to them. They fear what you will do to their family. You have won nothing here."

"We won the fight," Mark said, disturbed at how much this man's words bothered him.

The bloodied man shook his head. "You spoke of rebuilding the world and allowing people to join you. But people cannot build anything that stands on foundations of fear and anger."

"The history of empires have always been founded on bodies," Mark answered. "I never said ours would be any different."

The bloodied man nodded. "I see. So you're building an empire? Then who do you serve?"

Mark frowned. "What are you talking about?"

"If you're building an empire, then you're building it for an emperor," he answered. "Empires typically don't bode well for the common man. There is no room for democracy in an empire. Because in an empire, the masses serve only one."

It wasn't just the man's words that frightened Mark, but how they deeply penetrated his thoughts and challenged his beliefs. It was like hearing somebody talk of science and reason after decades of being lost in the dark ages. Mark imagined that the Renaissance was something like what he was feeling right now. A bit of light was shining through a crack in the door that had been closed longer than he could remember. And now, his curiosity was pulling him toward that light to see what else he could find.

"Sir," the scout said. "We need to finish this."

Mark turned and looked back down at the man who still couldn't open his eyes. He knelt in front of the man and then wiped the blood from his eyes. The man blinked repeatedly, and once he could finally see, Mark waited until the man was focused on him.

"You're not what I thought you'd look like," the man said.

"I never am," Mark replied. "You think you might understand what we are, but I can assure you that you don't. This country has been plagued with sickness, and we are the cure."

"I wouldn't call this a cure," the bloodied man said. "Maybe genocide or murder."

Mark's anger boiled over as he reached for his sidearm. He stood and aimed the pistol down at the man. "You speak like a man who was born on his knees, and now you will die on your knees."

"No," he said. "I was born a free man, in a free country, and that's exactly how I'll go." He struggled, wiggling from side to side, and then finally stood on a pair of shaking legs. "I'll die on my feet, in my hometown, in my country. Because you haven't won this war yet. And if this is the way that you're treating the folks you come across, I can promise you that you will never win this fight."

Ben's voice was now screaming in Mark's head. And as Mark raised the pistol and aimed it at the man's head, he felt a cold sense of dread overtake his senses. Because deep down, he knew this man was right. No matter how much death and destruction they brought upon the country, they could not eradicate everything by force. If they couldn't win the hearts of the people they wished to build a new country for, then there was no hope for their movement to gain momentum. And if they couldn't have people in their country, then what the hell were they fighting for?

"You still have a choice," the bloodied man said.

"So do you," Mark said.

The man nodded and then tilted his chin upward and straightened his posture. He wasn't going to change his mind, but Mark suddenly had a feeling that he might be changing his own.

"Do it," the scout said, growing angry behind Mark. "What are you waiting for? Just smoke the damn bastard."

Mark placed his finger on the trigger, but he felt his arm beginning to shake. He knew what would happen if he didn't pull the trigger. The men would turn on him, and every sacrifice he had made, all of the pain that he had endured would've been for nothing. Because while he had never been afraid to die for the cause he had joined, he was afraid of dying for a cause he no longer believed in.

"It's not too late," the bloodied man said.

Mark desperately wanted to believe this stranger, but he knew the truth. And it didn't matter how loud his brother's voice grew in his head, and it didn't matter how many people tried to come after him. He wasn't going to break, no matter what kind of hell he might be creating for himself.

"Think about—"

Mark pulled the trigger and the man collapsed to the pavement. The rest of the men on their knees remained quiet, and Mark stepped back as he gestured to the scout. "No survivors."

The scout nodded, and Mark eyed the sniveling cowards on the ground, kneeling before them. He would not be thrown off course by these weaklings. He would rise above this to reinstate himself and become one of the strongest individuals The New Order had ever seen.

And as his men carried out his orders, Mark listened to the screams of people begging for mercy. He made sure to listen closely because he had no intention of ever waning in his support of their mission ever again. No matter what it would cost his soul.

---

8

*J*ane watched as Ben rode off with the military man. She found it interesting how often he'd been gone lately, but she could use that to her advantage. If she were going to paint the Rikers as the irresponsible pair, Ben's absence would be a good point to showcase. Nothing was as effective in smearing someone's character than using the truth. And the truth was that Ben's absence was causing a strain on the rest of the community.

"Hey," Lester said, sneaking up behind her. "Danny came back. He says he wants to talk to us."

"Where the hell has he been?" Jane asked.

"He didn't say," Lester said.

Jane didn't like how Danny had been so secretive. If she were going to move against the Rikers, she needed to get her entire family on board. She didn't think Danny would be a problem, but at the very least, he needed to stick around long enough to hear the plan.

"Any luck with Gray?" Lester asked.

Jane shook her head. "Last I saw him, he was thanking Ben Riker for saving his life. I swear sometimes I think that boy wishes he had a different family."

Lester stopped and stood in front of Jane. "Don't talk like that. This is his family. We just need to remind him who the real enemy is."

"And who is that enemy?" Jane asked. "Because our son seems to think it's us."

"You will get him to come around," Lester answered. "You love him too much, and deep down, he still loves you, even though he's too stubborn to show it right now."

Lester placed his arm around Jane as they returned to their portable. Danny was already inside, waiting for them, and Jane was curious what he had been up to.

"You know how you told me to keep an eye out for things that might help us?" Danny asked.

Jane nodded and then crossed her arms. "Yeah."

Danny held up his hands and then retreated toward the back of the portable. "All right, but before you freak out, give me a minute to explain. Okay?"

Jane couldn't imagine what Danny had brought back to show them, but she never would have imagined what stepped from the back of the portable.

It had been so dark, and Jane was so distracted by Danny that she didn't even realize there was a person in the portable with them. And while the man stepped forward covered in darkness, it didn't take long for Jane to recognize the face of the stranger Danny had brought them.

"You son of a bitch!" Lester lunged forward, but Danny intercepted him, holding him back. All the while, the man Lester tried to attack never flinched. "How could you bring him here? What the hell were you thinking?"

While Lester fought with his brother over their new guest, Jane remained frozen in shock. It had been a long time since she'd seen him. And while she had only met him a handful of times, each encounter was memorable.

Buford Percy, Lester and Danny's father, stood motionless in the back of the room. He was a large man, more muscle than his two boys. Jane had always assumed that Lester and Danny took after their mother when it came to their lean frame because Buford Percy was built like a tank. And his time in prison over the past twenty years had only made him larger.

"Hello, son," Buford said.

Lester eventually shoved Danny off of him, aiming an accusatory finger at his estranged father. "You shouldn't be here."

"I know this is difficult for you," Buford said. "Even I'm surprised to see you. But circumstances have allowed an early release for my time incarcerated."

Lester paced around like an angry tiger. "Well, I

don't have any problem taking you back to prison and throwing away the key."

Buford only nodded and then bowed his head. He clasped his hands in front of him, and Jane saw the tattoos scrawled around his forearms. He looked even more menacing than what she remembered. And when he turned his gaze onto Jane, she felt that tingly sensation of fear crawl up her spine.

"Jane," Buford said, his voice deep but welcoming, "it's good to see you again."

"What are you doing here?" Jane asked, her voice incredibly dry. She wasn't sure she would be able to get the words out.

"I brought him," Danny said. "I found him on my ranging to the north when I was hunting deer."

"He nearly shot me when I stepped out from the bushes," Buford said and then laughed. "You always had a good eye, Danny. I appreciate you not pulling the trigger."

"Yeah, well, it would have been different if I had been there," Lester said. "That's for damned sure."

"I guess I should be glad he was hunting alone," Buford said.

Jane knew that Lester and Danny had a history with their father. The man had been the local drunk when they were children, but he also had a penchant for felonies. It was Buford Percy who had been the worst his family had to offer, and Lester and Danny had never been able to crawl out from beneath his shadow.

If circumstances had been different for Lester and Danny growing up, Jane suspected they really could have been something.

But one fatal accident changed the course of both Lester and Danny, and Ben Riker. It had been Buford Percy that was drunk and behind the wheel, causing the crash that killed Ben Riker's parents and imprisoned Burford.

"That doesn't answer the question," Jane said, her shock thawing, and she stepped forward. "Why are you here?"

"I told him about what we're trying to do," Danny said. "He thinks it's a good idea, and he wants to help."

"Help himself, you mean," Lester said. "That's all he's ever done, Danny. You think prison changed him? If anything, it made him worse!"

"I know you have your doubts about me, Lester," Buford said. "You have every right to hate me. But fate has brought us a new opportunity. There are no more criminal records, no more authority to track us down, nothing but what you're strong enough to take. It's like living in the old days, where fortune favors the strong. And you are strong. All of you are."

Jane knew that Buford Percy was a formidable man. But she had never been intimidated by him, even after all the stories Lester had told her about his childhood. Because Jane had been through hell herself growing up. Buford Percy might've been a mean son of a bitch, but he wasn't the devil.

"And so you come here to help us," Jane said though she remained skeptical. "How do you expect to do that?"

"I have developed quite a following during my time in prison," Buford answered. "After the power turned off, I managed to get a group of men and me out of our cells."

"Well," Lester said, taking a few steps forward, "let me save you a lot of time and frustration and tell you that you can get the hell out of here. We don't need your help. We don't *want* your help."

"I understand your hesitation in trusting me," Buford said. "But I think with our combined strength, we could become unstoppable. Think about it, Lester. Our family has been spit on for generations. This is our opportunity to take back everything that we lost. This could be our one chance at redemption. What else could it be other than fate for this to happen now? We shouldn't waste the future that's been handed to us on a silver platter."

"That's certainly a beautiful sentiment," Jane said, speaking up for her husband before he said anything more detrimental to their cause. "But running with a bunch of ex-cons isn't exactly going to change the image of the Percy family, is it?"

"A lot of my guys didn't do anything but burglary," Buford said. "They might have a temper, but they aren't killers. They are reliable guys who are trying to find their way just like us."

"You're so full of shit," Lester said. "You'd say anything to get us to agree to this."

Buford frowned. "You don't think I've changed? What was stopping me from marching over to this place the moment I found out who was here and what you guys are doing? You're not the only ones with bones to pick against the Riker family. I definitely have more fighting men than you do, and it wouldn't take very long to find some weapons to take you guys out. I could have overrun this place, but I chose to come to speak with you first. I don't want to be your enemy."

"A little too late for that," Lester said.

Jane knew how much her husband hated his father. She wasn't privy to the complete complicated history of the relationship, but she knew enough to know that Lester wasn't going to budge on his feelings about his father, but this was an opportunity that Jane could use to their advantage if she could get Lester on board.

"Buford, why don't you step outside for a second while we discuss this as a family," Jane said.

Lester immediately turned toward Jane, and she could see the shock and betrayal in his face. The fact that Jane even wanted to discuss this meant that she was considering keeping him around, and Lester found that unacceptable.

"I can sneak him back into the woods," Danny said.

Danny checked to make sure the coast was clear, and then collected Buford. As the big man moved past both of them, Jane could have cut the tension in the small space with a knife. But the moment Buford was gone, and it was only Jane and Lester, Jane knew that her husband was relieved he no longer had to be in the same room as his father.

"I can't believe what you're doing," Lester said, shaking his head.

"We have to look at this from every angle," Jane said. "We could use Buford to our advantage, and if he has the numbers he says he does, that will tip the scales in our favor."

Lester laughed. "You can't trust him. He will say anything and do anything to get what he wants."

"And what do you think he wants?" Jane asked.

"I don't know," Lester shrugged and flapped his arms at his sides. He paced nervously back and forth in short strides. "All I know is every time he's gotten involved in my life, it's taken a turn for the worse."

Jane chose her next words very carefully. She didn't want to push Lester too far over the edge to the point where they couldn't agree on anything. They needed to be a united front on this, or it wasn't going to work.

"We can still dictate terms," Jane said. "We put whatever demands we see fit on the table and see what he does? There's no harm in trying to figure out what it is that they can offer us."

Lester shook his head, but he wasn't as angry as before. "I don't know, Jane. I've spent my entire life living in that man's shadow, and I'm not in the mood to get back underneath it now. I wanted to build a new life with you, just us, together. Anything we do with my father will be tainted by him. I know it will."

Jane walked over to reach for her husband's hand, and she could barely wrap her entire hand around one of his fingers. It was times like this she was always reminded how small she really was compared to him and the rest of the world. She was a petite woman, but she had a fire in her that was only matched by the man standing in front of her. It was time to harness that potential.

"You are better than him," Jane said. "Better than him in every way. And if he even thinks of trying to double-cross us, we will shut him down. You're not a boy anymore. He does not have any sway over what you do. And if he crosses you, then you will put him in his place. That is the greatest revenge you could ever take against him."

"If we do this," Lester said, "the moment he tries to pull any type of shit, we need to shut it down. All of us, including Danny.

Jane nodded. "Of course. We wouldn't do it any other way."

Once Danny returned from the woods, Jane and Lester brought him up to speed on their thoughts. It didn't take much convincing for Danny, he had been a yes from the beginning, but Jane made sure Danny understood the conditions.

"No more sneaking around," Jane said. "The fact that you didn't tell us about this has eroded some of our trust. And trust is the only thing we have right now."

Danny avoided Jane's eyes, staring at the floor. "I didn't know any other way to get you guys to meet with him." When Danny finally looked up, he turned to his brother. "I know what he did to us. I was there through it all with you. But we're not scared little boys anymore. We can make our own way now. And we can do that together."

Now that everybody was on board, all Jane had to do was hammer out the specifics of their deal. Danny led them out into the woods, where they found Buford waiting.

Jane decided to allow Lester to lay down the law when it came to his father. It was important for him to make it clear what their boundaries were and who was in charge. And Jane knew this was a big confidence booster for Lester, which would help him in his relationship with his father.

"You don't do anything without our say-so," Lester said. "Anytime we tell you to do something, you do it immediately, no questions asked. We're not here to create a partnership. You would be working for us, along with all of the men that you bring with you."

Buford rubbed his jaw and nodded along. "I don't have a problem with those conditions, but my guys might have some things to say about it."

Jane rolled her eyes. "And what do think your 'guys' would object to?"

"I don't know, but we could go and ask them," Buford answered. "They're not very far from here, and I know they would probably feel more comfortable meeting you all." He stopped himself and then immediately turned to Lester. "If that's okay with you, of course."

Jane studied her husband. He was out of his element when it came to dealing with negotiations, and it seemed that Buford was well versed. He was playing Lester like a fiddle. But that was what Jane was here for, to help keep Lester on track.

"I think that would be fine," Lester said, but even as he spoke, he turned back toward Jane and saw his wife shake her head, and then he quickly changed his tune. "But first, we need to make sure your people aren't armed."

"We only have a few weapons among us," Buford said. "But we can set them aside in order to talk this through."

Jane approached Lester's side and whispered in his ear, "I think they should come here."

Jane thought that having Buford's people be the ones to travel here would put them in a position of power. And if things turned south, they would have a quick retreat to the facility.

"Bring your guys here," Lester said, parroting what Jane told in. "Then we will talk."

Buford nodded and then disappeared into the woods.

"What do we do if they decide to get violent?" Lester asked. "If he has as many guys as he says he does, it wouldn't take much for him to mow us down."

"If they start getting out of hand, we're close enough to the facility to call for backup," Jane said.

"I thought the point of this was to make sure the facility didn't know what we were doing," Danny said.

"The point of this is to build a case against the Rikers and put us in a position of power," Jane said. "It doesn't matter how that happens. We need a common enemy. If your father decides to attack us at this point, then he becomes the common enemy. By the time the dust settles on what happened, it won't matter who Buford was or his association with this family. We'll have defended people against a very violent and vicious attack."

"So either way, we end up on top," Danny said.

"Yeah," Lester said. "So long as we're still alive to see the victory."

When Buford finally returned with the rest of his people, Jane confirmed that Buford was at least telling the truth about the number of people he'd bought.

At first glance, Jane could immediately tell that all of them had been in prison. Despite Buford's claim that these weren't violent offenders, each of them had a hardness to them that suggested otherwise. It was the kind of people Jane remembered seeing around her growing up. But whether or not they could back up those tough glances remained to be seen.

"Lester, Jane, Danny," Buford said. "These are the guys." He gestured to the fifteen men who remained scattered in the woods.

Most of the prisoners still wore their prison jumpsuits, but Buford had somehow managed to score some clothing along the journey.

"I hope you're not attached to those uniforms," Jane said. "Because I don't expect them to do you much good for what we have planned."

"What *we* have planned?" one of the inmates said. "I don't remember agreeing to any plan."

"Take it easy, Jimmy," Buford said.

Jimmy was a bruiser of a man, complete with a fat shaved head, shoulders the size of boulders, and a barrel of a midsection, complemented by a pair of tiny, beady eyes, that made him look like a henchman from a comic book.

"That's what we're here to discuss," Buford said. "I've caught the boys up to speed, but we think we have a more aggressive approach to getting things done."

"Yeah," Jimmy said. "We go in and take over the fucking place." He laughed, and it triggered more chuckles from the rest of the crew.

"That's not the option we're going with," Lester said, standing his ground, which immediately put Jimmy and the rest of the goons on the defensive. "We're working on trying to make a play for control, and the only way to do that is to make sure that we're not the bad guys."

"You do realize everybody here was recently imprisoned, right?" Jimmy asked. "If you wanted a bunch of good guys, you should have recruited the local precinct."

Jane could tell this was a situation that would only become more volatile the longer they remained out here, so she stepped in to help. "Taking the facility by force is out of the question," Jane said. "We are living in a world where if you want to control people, you need to have their trust. And breaking down someone's front door isn't the way they were going to earn their trust."

"We do it their way, or we don't do it all," Buford said. "Nobody is forcing anybody to be here. If you don't like the deal, you can always walk away."

The group was silent for a little while, mulling over the options before tiny-eyed Jimmy stepped forward and started making threats. "And why would we listen to anything you have to say?" Jimmy asked. "What's to stop us from marching past you and taking what we want."

Buford stepped forward. "Me. Do I make myself clear?"

Jimmy stood his ground for only a few minutes before he retreated. The rest of the inmates Buford had brought with him followed suit, and now that everyone was under control, Buford turned to his oldest son.

"We will follow your lead on this," Buford said. "Whatever you think is best."

Jane found it curious that Buford was so willing to agree to whatever demands they had set forth, but it appeared that his loyalty to Lester and Danny bought him some goodwill where before he'd had none. But what Buford would use that goodwill for Jane needed to find out. And she needed to find out before Buford destroyed her family.

9

---

*N*ancy did a recount of the number of bodies they had at the facility. Sixteen women had followed them from the women's clinic when she and Sarah were searching for medicine for Kurt and Susan's baby. All of the portables at the facility were already taken. And after Nancy and Sarah had spoken with everybody who currently occupied those portables, nobody was comfortable in continuing to share their limited space.

"Those tents aren't going to do them any good once it starts getting cold and rainy," Sarah said, staring out at the field of tents they had set up. The facility had a stash of camping gear they had managed to use and set up as a temporary fix for all the extra people. But everyone was growing tired of the temporary housing, and she and Nancy had been tasked with finding a permanent solution.

"Well, until people are comfortable with having some roommates, I don't know how we are going to change that," Nancy said. "I'm not exactly the construction aficionado."

"Building some habitable housing doesn't have to be fancy or extravagant," Sarah said. "I did some work with Habitat for Humanity for my engineering degree. So long as people are open to the interpretation for the word house, I think we could make something work with materials we find from the city."

"Could you really make something like that work?" Nancy asked.

Sarah remained focused on the field of tents where the women were currently idle. She cocked her jaw to the side and chewed on the inside of her cheek. "I'm not sure we have much of a choice. If people continue to get antsy and uncomfortable in this place, then the mood will become volatile. The last thing we need is another coup on our hands."

"Doesn't Habitat for Humanity have people help them build the houses that they're going to live in?" Nancy asked.

Sarah nodded. "Yeah, and I thought our new friends could pitch in."

Nancy had been watching some of the women they had brought back. They were very timid, small things. They looked incredibly weak and fragile, but she wasn't much different than them when she had first arrived here. It had taken time for her to grow into the skills she now possessed. And with a little time and training, those women could do the same.

"Well," Nancy said. "I guess we need to go deliver the good news."

Sarah laughed. "Hopefully, they won't see it as forced, unpaid labor."

"They might not say anything," Nancy said. "But I plan to file a few grievances."

Sarah shoved Nancy in the arm, and the pair started to walk over to the women. The nurse who had come back with them, the woman who had run the clinic, Shelby, had become their official spokesperson.

"Hey, girls," Shelby said. "What's up?"

"Well, we know the living situation hasn't been ideal for you and the other women," Sarah said. "But we had a few ideas that we wanted to run by you."

Shelby smiled. "I think anything would be better than what we have, but I suppose beggars can't be choosers. I'll gather the ladies."

Nancy and Sarah hung back while Shelby made the rounds. The woman emerged from their tents, looking as though they had slept most of the day. Despite the rest of the facility having been assigned work, Mrs. Riker hadn't gotten around to getting any of these women jobs. It was starting to upset the rest of the community who were working shifts to keep this place running.

"Okay, ladies," Shelby said. "Nancy and Sarah

wanted to run a few things by us in regards to our living situation, so let's hear them out."

Shelby gestured to Sarah, who stepped forward. While Nancy might have become more comfortable handling weapons and learning how to fight, public speaking wasn't her strong suit. She was thankful Sarah was willing to take on that role.

"I know the living situation here hasn't been ideal for everyone," Sarah said. "But my family and I appreciate you making do with what we are able to give you."

"How come we can't be in one of those portables?" one of the women asked.

A few grumbles from the other women echoed a similar sentiment, and Nancy felt the shift in the meeting growing toward an unfavorable outcome.

"We're working on a more permanent solution," Sarah answered, trying to find her footing in the conversation. "And I think we've come up with something that will—"

"Are you the one in charge?" another woman asked.

Sarah was thrown off guard, and she stuttered in her reply. "Um, I don't think—I'm in charge of finding you better accommodations."

"But who runs the facility?" another woman asked, and again it triggered another echo of murmurs.

"My parents," Sarah answered. "Liz and Ben Riker."

"And where are they?" the first woman from before asked. "Because it seems to me that looking for housing shouldn't be the responsibility of two kids."

Nancy knew this conversation wasn't going anywhere. The tide was turning even harder in the wrong direction for a productive outcome. Still, to Sarah's credit, she stood her ground, and that caused Nancy to stick around.

"Ladies, please!" Sarah raised her voice, upping her intensity. "I understand your frustration. But none of you are being forced to stay here." She looked out among the crowd, and the fervor died down a little bit. "We have provided you food, shelter, and protection. Has it been hard? Of course, it has, but look around! The world has changed, and we need to change with it if we want to survive. We can't sit around and wait for something to come to us. We must go out and find it."

The murmurs continued, but this time Nancy saw most of the women nodding in agreement.

"There you go, Sarah," Nancy said, whispering to herself.

"I was an engineering major before all of this happened, and I did some work with Habitat for Humanity," Sarah said. "I think I can help construct a more permanent solution for everyone if we manage to find the right materials. And when I say *we*, I mean all of you." She gestured out to the women. "If you want to improve your situation, then you all need to start pulling your weight. Anyone willing to come with Nancy and me to the city to look for supplies and actually help us put something together will be offered a place to stay in what we build. Everyone who doesn't help—" Sarah gestured to the tents around them— "Looks like you'll be roughing it for a little while longer." She dropped her hands and then turned around and walked away, leaving the women to chat amongst themselves.

Nancy caught up with Sarah, smiling. "Hell of a speech."

"Yeah, well, I was winging it, so…" Sarah shrugged. "You think I turned them off?"

"I think you lit a fire under their asses," Nancy said. "Hell, I think I'm ready to build my own house."

Sarah chuckled. "Well, we need to find the materials first. I think if we start—"

"Nancy?"

Both girls turned around to find Carolina jogging after them. She was wheezing by the time she caught up with them, and she hunched forward to catch her breath. When she lifted her head, her cheeks were still flushed red.

"What's up?" Nancy asked.

"I just wanted to—whew, sorry." Carolina took another deep breath, and she was finally back to normal. "I just wanted to see if I could learn a few things from you."

"Learn what?" Nancy asked.

Carolina pointed to the rifle on Nancy's arm. "I saw you practicing the other day with that thing, and I thought maybe I could try it out." She pointed to the other women behind them. "I think it would be helpful for the other women as well. Maybe you could show us a few pointers?"

Nancy had never considered herself a teacher, and since most of the women from the clinic were twice her age, she didn't even think any of them would want to learn from her simply because she was so young. Still, she wasn't sure if she was ready to take on something like that. She was just now starting to get the hang of everything herself.

"But if you can't, I understand," Carolina said, quickly shutting herself down before Nancy even had a chance to reply.

Carolina's disappointment was evident as she looked away, and Nancy immediately felt guilty for even considering keeping her skills to herself. Here was a woman who needed a way to protect herself from violence, and Nancy was withholding the key that could unlock a whole new world for her.

"Yes," Nancy said. "I can show you guys a few pointers. Some simple techniques that I think would be useful for everybody."

Carolina's smile brightened, but she tried to downplay her excitement. "Okay, great. I will go back and let the other ladies know." She looked to Sarah, still smiling. "I agree with what you said, by the way. I think it's time for all of us to start pulling our own weight. I know a lot of the other girls feel that way, too, just so you know."

"Well then, I hope to see everybody join us for our trip down to the city," Sarah said.

Carolina waved goodbye and then jogged back over to the tents where the rest of the women waited. Nancy watched the other women's reaction when she told them the news and saw how excited everybody was. It made Nancy both nervous and excited herself because now she needed to figure out how to teach all of these women everything that she had learned herself. She hoped the women were better students than she was.

Before Nancy turned around, she saw Willie step out of his tent. He saw Carolina speaking with the other women, and the moment he saw how happy she was, he immediately scowled. He marched over quickly and pulled her arm, yanking her away from the other women.

When Nancy saw how angry Willie was and how he was shoving his finger in her face, Nancy found herself moving toward the pair with her rifle at the ready. The closer she moved toward them, the easier it was to hear their conversation.

"I was just talking with them," Carolina said, her voice sheepish.

"I don't need you speaking with those women, getting ideas in your head," Willie said. "Now get back in the tent."

"Is there a problem here?" Nancy asked.

Willie immediately turned his angry glare at Nancy. Until now, Willie had been nothing but mischievously playful toward her. But this was the first time Nancy had caught Willie's real face. This was the first time she saw his anger.

"This is none of your business," Willie said. "So go and mind your own."

Before Willie could turn around, Nancy blocked his path, again keeping her rifle at the ready.

Willie snarled. "Move. Now."

Nancy realized that if she backed down, it would set a dangerous precedent for Willie, and Nancy didn't want his confidence to gain any momentum. If this was going to be their moment of confrontation, then so be it. Nancy wasn't about to let Willie intimidate her in front of the women that she was about to teach self-defense classes. This should be their first lesson.

"Hey!" Sarah came up from behind Willie, aiming her pistol at him. "Why don't you take a step back?"

Willie glanced back at Sarah and then looked to Nancy. He was in a bad position, and he knew it. He held up his hands and hid some of his anger, but he couldn't get rid of all of it. "Just a simple misunderstanding."

Nancy shook her head. "I don't think there is any misunderstanding on my end. I think you were going to try to hurt Carolina. And I was in the way of stopping it."

Willie chortled and noticed how more eyes were watching them. If he made a move, he would be ousted from the community without prejudice. There would be no way to salvage any type of plausible deniability. And if Willie were as smart as Nancy thought he was, he wouldn't risk wasting his one move on this silly spat.

Willie raised his hands passively and removed himself from the situation. "I think you got me all wrong, Nancy. I'm just going to take a walk." He reached into his pocket and removed a packet of cigarettes and a lighter. "I just want to take a quick smoke break, boss." That easy-going charm returned for one final flash of a smile before he turned around and quickly walked away from the tents and the other women.

Sarah joined Nancy, lowering her weapon. "You all right?"

Nancy nodded. "He's going to hurt her again. He's got a lot of stuff building up, and when it explodes, it's going to be bad."

Sarah sighed. "I wish we could just kick him out. But my dad says it's better to keep an eye on him instead of having him out there as a threat."

"Yeah," Nancy said dryly. "It's much better for him to be a threat on the inside."

Nancy turned to the other women and tried to gauge their reactions. All of them looked nervous, but none of them had spoken out against Willie since they had arrived. Either they were all afraid of him, or he really had been staying out of trouble.

"Sarah, Nancy." Mrs. Riker jogged up to them, and

the moment Nancy saw Mrs. Riker's expression, she knew that something was wrong. "I need you both to come with me. Keep quiet, and don't make it look like we're causing a scene."

Nancy and Sarah exchanged a quick glance before following Mrs. Riker away from the tents and the rest of the women.

Nancy and Sarah walked on either side of Mrs. Riker as they headed toward the main building. Nancy hadn't ever seen Mrs. Riker this worried unless there was a legitimate crisis. And the last crisis they had dealt with was an attack on the facility. But as Nancy glanced out around the surrounding area through the fence line, she couldn't see any immediate threat.

"What's going on?" Sarah asked.

"We have a situation back in the kitchen," Mrs. Riker said. "I will explain when we get inside and we can speak privately."

Nancy didn't like Mrs. Riker's tone, and she was worried about what they would find when they entered the mess hall.

The mess hall was empty inside, and Nancy and Sarah followed Mrs. Riker into the kitchen and toward the food storage locker. At first, Nancy thought something had happened with Abe, but when they passed his locker without stopping and saw him inside, she was relieved. And then she was unsure of what to make about her feeling relieved.

Eventually, Mrs. Riker stopped at the storage cooler

where they kept all their dried goods. It was there she saw Cole, who she knew was Sarah's biological father, pacing back and forth in front of the big cooler area. It wasn't until Nancy looked inside the cooler and she saw what was missing that she understood the crisis at hand.

"Oh my God," Sarah said.

This morning the cooler had been stocked full of provisions. Wheat, grains, canned foods, and the rest of the MRE rations stored at the facility. But now, the storage area was only half full of what it had been earlier today.

"What the hell happened?" Sarah asked. "Were we robbed?"

Mrs. Riker was staring at Cole, and Nancy could see the anger radiating off of her. "That's what we're trying to figure out. Because apparently guarding the food doesn't necessarily mean guarding it all of the time."

"I was gone for a couple minutes," Cole said. "I was helping Rachel with something."

Mrs. Riker shook her head, disgusted, and it took Sarah and Nancy a moment to realize what that "something" really meant.

"Eww, Dad, what the hell?" Sarah asked.

"Hey, don't use that kind of language," Cole answered, but his parental chops didn't provide him with a leg to stand on.

"How much is gone?" Nancy asked.

"Almost half," Mrs. Riker answered.

"It would have taken more than one person to do this," Sarah said. "Unless you were gone for like an hour, in which case, more gross, Dad."

"Look, they couldn't have gotten far," Cole said. "All we have to do is search everyone's portable, get the food back, and then we'll be good to go. It's not like there are a lot of hiding places at the facility. And we have a key to get into every room we need to."

"I don't like the idea of intruding on people's privacy," Mrs. Riker said. "But we need to recover the food quickly before we miss our chance to get it back."

Mrs. Riker rubbed her forehead, and Nancy could tell that she was stressed. But who wouldn't be under the current circumstances?

"The faster we get this done, the easier it will be to control the damage," Mrs. Riker said.

"I'm sure it's going to be fine—" Cole stopped when he saw the daggers in Mrs. Riker's eyes boring into him. He didn't dare move save for the one step he took backward.

"I don't think you understand how thin the line is that we're walking here," Mrs. Riker said. "We have double the amount of people we had when this food storage was here. Food is our stability. If that disappears, then so does people's civility."

"We should start knocking on doors," Nancy said. "I think I might have an idea of where we start."

"Who?" Sarah asked.

"The Percy's," Nancy answered. "This has their fingerprints all over it."

"That doesn't make any sense," Sarah said. "They made a deal with us. And we still have the numbers against them if they were to try anything aggressive."

"Trust me when I tell you that those people are capable of anything," Nancy said. "They will do whatever it takes to save their own skin."

"We will get to the Percy's eventually," Mrs. Riker said. "Right now, it's important for us to remain calm and not to cause panic."

"Well, we're going to have to tell people we're looking for when we search their things, right?" Sarah said. "So how do you tell them that half of our food is missing without causing a panic?"

"We try to do it all once," Mrs. Riker answered. "Each of us can take a section of the facility, and by the time people realize what's happening, hopefully, we'll have found the food by then."

"And if we don't find the food?" Nancy asked.

"We will cross that bridge when we come to it," Mrs. Riker answered.

Once assignments were divvied out, the four of them begin their search of the facility. But before Nancy started searching her own area, she made a pit stop to speak to Abe and explained what happened.

Abe's eyes widened. "Half?"

"Yeah," Nancy answered. "You hear anything down here? Or see somebody come by?"

Abe shook his head. "I guess I fell asleep on duty."

If Abe hadn't seen anybody come through, then either he had been asleep, or the thieves had entered through the back door where she would come through to see Abe.

"What is it?" Abe asked. "You look worried."

"None of this makes any sense," Nancy answered. "For somebody to steal that much food, you would think they were going to leave with it. But that amount of food would require a huge wagon and several people to transport it."

"And?" Abe asked.

"My point is that it would be difficult to hide," Nancy answered. "Anyone with half a brain would realize that. If their goal were to steal food, it would have made more sense to steal a little bit at a time, try to keep it under the radar. And it wasn't like people weren't being fed here on a timely and regular basis. Whoever did this wanted to make a statement."

"Do you have an idea of who it might be?" he asked.

Nancy nodded. But she hadn't been tasked with searching the Percy's belongings. But she would bet her life that those people had something to do this. She just needed to prove it.

There wasn't much conversation on the road with Jackson. But Ben didn't mind the silence. Both men were frustrated with one another.

The horses trotted at a leisurely pace through the woods. It had been Ben's suggestion that they stay off the main highways as much as possible. Ben did not want to run into a scenario where they found themselves in a fight and outmanned.

"Are we getting close?" Jackson asked.

"It should only be another few miles," Ben answered. "So long as we stay on this path, we should run right into it."

"Okay then." Jackson nodded. "I don't like the idea of us going into this without clearing the air." He adjusted himself in the saddle, which he looked uncomfortable in.

Ben didn't think the man had spent much time on

horseback during his life.

"I never go into a war zone unless I trust the man around me absolutely." He looked to Ben with intensity. "Did you kill Beckett?"

Ben held the colonel's gaze. "I didn't kill your man." He cleared his throat. "It was my brother."

Jackson frowned. "Your brother? Did I meet him back at the facility?"

"No," Ben answered. "My brother is part of The New Order. I hadn't seen him in almost a decade. He tracked me to my facility after I rescued my daughter from one of the prison camps. I didn't even know it was him until the very last second."

Ben hoped that the omission of truth about his brother would build trust between them. And judging from Jackson's expression, Ben's gamble had paid off.

"You're really serious about that, aren't you?" Jackson asked.

"I wish I wasn't," Ben answered. "But it's the truth. He came to my camp and kidnapped my daughter. He nearly killed me, and I almost killed him."

"So he got away," Jackson said, and then he shifted in the saddle again. "That's why you want backup from the military. You think he's going to come back with more people."

"I don't know what to think," Ben said. "The only thing matters to me now is making sure that my family is safe. And if getting the military involved helps accomplish that goal, then so be it."

Jackson was silent, and their conversation faded into the clicks of the horse's hooves and their soft breathing and occasional whinny. Ben thought maybe he had said too much but then Jackson broke the silence.

"Family is a hell of a thing," Jackson said. "I imagine there are quite a few people who have brothers and sisters, uncles and fathers, friends who have joined this organization. For so long, our country has been divided by hateful rhetoric. And it appears that the time for talking is over. It's a shame." He looked to Ben. "I'm sorry."

"And I'm sorry about your man," Ben said.

When they were less than a mile away from the supposed camp stationed in Eustis, Ben and Jackson tied off the horses, leaving them behind. They figured that the enemy camp would have guards on duty and wanted to sneak up unnoticed, a task much easier to complete without a horse.

The town of Eustis was small with a population of fewer than one hundred people and was nothing more than a few buildings and a single stoplight along the highway. But on the town's outskirts was a trailer park where Ben figured the town had earned most of its money. It was positioned in the middle of a few major cities and provided an overnight stay for anybody who was RVing or towing a trailer.

When Ben and Jackson found the town empty, Ben figured the operation was in the RV park, and when they approached, they saw the security stationed around the perimeter.

"How many guys, you think?" Ben asked.

Jackson studied the perimeter, giving it some thought. "I see five, and they probably have a reserve station somewhere, so it could be double that. Not to mention the guys they probably have watching the workers in each of those trailers."

Ben counted at least a dozen trailers scattered across the open lot. There weren't many trees and foliage, which made sneaking around the place that much more difficult.

"We need to find a way in and figure out exactly what's inside those trailers," Ben said.

"We should hang back for a few minutes and get a feel for their security," Jackson said. "If we can figure out when they made it past, we can figure out how to time it so we can evade their guards."

Ben and Jackson waited, watching how the security team would navigate the trailer park. They seemed to stick to the perimeter, but every once in a while, a man would come out of the portables and relieve one of the guys outside. If they didn't relieve anybody, they went to the trailer in the center of the lot. Ben figured that was where the sleeping quarters were for the guards.

Once they had the paths down, with the exception of the random guard stepping out of the portables, Ben and Jackson readied themselves.

"I know you can handle yourself with a weapon,"

Jackson said. "But we're not going inside guns blazing. Understand that, right?"

"Stealth is definitely the way to go," Ben answered. "I don't have a problem with that."

Jackson checked his pistol, making sure everything was loaded. "Listen, when you're in the heat of battle, it can be easier to kill a man. There's a lot of things happening all at once. But have you ever been in a situation where you killed somebody quietly?"

Ben had already killed more people than he had ever wanted to, but he knew these were extreme circumstances. The only thing that could make this worse was the fact that he had to kill someone who hadn't engaged in any violence with him.

"I thought you said we shouldn't cause a scene," Ben said.

"I said we shouldn't go in guns blazing," Jackson replied. "Look, the only reason I ask is in order for this recon mission to work, we might have to put some guys out of their misery. In order to do that, we'll need to make sure we don't fire our weapons."

Ben reached for the blade on his pant leg. "I understand." Ben always believed in preparing for the worst-case scenario. It was the reason he was so attracted to prepping. It gave him the tools necessary to make sure that he could survive with his family. It offered a layer of protection, a buffer to a world that cared nothing about your well-being.

But he knew no amount of preparation could

prepare him for sneaking up behind a man and killing him in cold blood.

However, Ben forced himself to remember what these people stood for. They had killed innocent civilians and had done irreparable harm to the country. They were a deadly enemy.

Once the guards had cleared their entry point, Ben and Jackson moved to the perimeter. There was a makeshift fence that surrounded the entire area, but it was easily maneuvered around. The barbed wire wasn't applied correctly to the barrier they had constructed, and after a few moments of snipping wires, they had cleared a path for themselves.

As Ben and Jackson neared the first trailer, they remained crouched, making sure no one from inside could see them. But as Ben glanced up at the window, he realized the windows were blocked over with newspapers, which didn't allow anyone to see inside.

But it also meant no one inside could see outside, either.

Ben nudged Jackson, pointing out what he found, and Jackson nodded. Ben never learned any of the military signs, but based on what Jackson was motioning with his hand, Ben determined that they would go inside this first trailer. Jackson would take the point, with Ben acting as backup.

Ben followed Jackson around the corner of the trailer as they approached the stairs to the door. Jackson leaned his ear against the door and listened inside. After a few seconds, he looked at Ben and nodded as he gripped the door handle. Ben stiffened, readying himself for whatever they encountered on the other side.

Between the moment Jackson opened the door and Ben stepping inside felt like an eternity. The world passed round in slow motion, and just when Ben thought he had missed something, Jackson shut the door behind them.

"It's empty," Jackson said.

Inside were five tables, each of them with parts and pieces of equipment that looked like it was a part of some type of engine. Ben had never been mechanically inclined, but he recognized a few pieces spread across the tables. He walked to the nearest one and picked up one of the dirtied metal pieces.

"Looks like an engine threw up in here," Jackson said, quickly scanning each table before moving on, and headed for the door. "What we're looking for isn't here."

But Ben remained by the table, continuing to study the parts.

"You remember the helicopter I told you about?" Ben asked.

"Yeah, the one you said your guy saw the day after the EMP," Jackson answered. "You're saying these are helicopter parts or something?"

"No," Ben answered. "But remember what Abe told us? They're rebuilding weapons, and transportation could be one of them. How valuable would a plane or a car be right now?"

Jackson nodded. "It makes sense. But I didn't see any vehicles in the area." He glanced around the inside of the trailer as if someone was listening. "We need to keep looking around. Until we find our big-ticket item, we don't stop moving."

The pair returned to the door. Jackson leaned against the wall as he cracked open the door and peered outside. Ben watched from the window, peeling back some of the newspaper so he could see as well.

Once they confirmed that the coast was clear, they hurried out of the trailer, ran around to the backside next to the woods, and started searching the rest of the area.

All the trailers and RVs they came across had their windows tinted, but it was clear which ones were filled with people and which ones were empty. The trailer and RV walls were very thin, and the conversations of the enemy could be heard outside.

The second trailer they examined was much like the first, empty save for some spare parts stored in it. But instead of engine parts, the second trailer consisted mostly of pieces of artillery weapons. Not just rifles and pistols, but the heavy-duty projectiles. Mortars that could crumble the wall of a concrete building and scnd it tumbling to the ground.

But what was more concerning was what they found in the third unoccupied trailer. It was a Class-C

RV, and it reminded Ben of the same RV they had used three summers ago to take the family cross-country trip to California. It had been one of his favorite trips, but Ben didn't know why that popped into his head.

Maybe it was because when he saw what was on the tables and hanging from the walls and ceiling terrified him, and it made him want to go and be with his family. Or maybe it was because he feared that the people he saw in the pictures were signs of his family's future.

Jackson reached for one of the photographs taped to the wall. A young man was stripped down, naked, with duct tape around his ankles and his wrists, both tied together behind his back. He lay on a slab of concrete curled up in the fetal position, and there was a puddle of blood behind his head.

It was like walking into a house of horrors, except instead of everyone playing pretend, it was all real.

"Dear God," Jackson said, looking at the other pictures. "They're all like this."

Every photograph had a different person in it, but they were all posed in the same posture. Ankles and wrists tied, stripped naked, and what looked like a bullet to the side of the head. They were all on the same concrete slab, which meant that they were all killed in the same location, most likely.

"What the hell are they doing?" Jackson asked.

Ben reached for another photograph and flipped it around to study the back. "There's writing on the back of these. This one has a name. Daniel Watson." He flipped the photograph around so Jackson could see it. "That name mean anything to you?"

Jackson shook his head. "I don't think I have ever seen any of these people in my life. And I would have been fine not seeing them like this."

Ben understood the sentiment, but he couldn't wrap his head around why The New Order had targeted these people? Were they high-ranking officials of some kind? Traitors who were made an example of?

Before Ben could figure out the answer, there was movement outside their RV. Both Jackson and Ben remained quiet, but Jackson positioned himself by the door. He moved a piece of the newspaper aside to get a better look at what was happening outside. Curious, Ben joined Jackson.

Two guards stood at the front of the trailer across from them, and the door was open. A third guard was inside, shouting something to another person, and after a minute of arguing, a man was shoved outside and thrown into the arms of the two guards standing at the bottom of the door.

All three guards whisked the man away, whose face was covered in bruises.

"We need to get inside that trailer," Jackson said.

"We don't know if there's anybody else inside," Ben said. "And we don't know when those guards are going to come back."

"All the more reason to figure out what was inside

and to do it quickly," Jackson said. "I'm going in there with or without you. If you want to stay here, then go ahead, just don't get yourself caught or killed."

Ben removed his hand from the door, and Jackson opened it. Knowing that it would be better if he saw whatever was inside firsthand, Ben followed Jackson into the second trailer.

Unlike the other trailers they had seen, there were no spare parts on tables, but instead, they found a series of drawings on large sheets of paper.

"What the hell are these?" Ben asked.

Jackson reached for the nearest sheet of paper. "Schematics. Technical readouts for something very advanced.

There were dozens of similar schematics posted all around the room, and on the end of the trailer was a desk, a big one like an architect would use to draw up a new building.

Jackson walked over to the table and saw the drawings the man had been working on. He flipped through them quickly, and by the time Ben stood by his side, he flattened all of them back on the table. He leaned forward, pressing his palm against the top stack of the papers, and closed his eyes.

"What is it?" Ben asked.

Jackson looked like he was about to vomit. "When I first joined the military, I was with a marine unit specializing in nuclear cleanup. We would be a first response team in the event of a nuclear fallout event to help clear and evacuated the area. Part of our training was to recognize other devices that could be still in the area and mark them to be defused." He opened his eyes and pressed his finger into the center of the schematics on the table. "This is a drawing of a nuclear device. Probably at least one-megaton blast. Small by today's modern standards, but still big enough to level a city. And still with enough radiation to poison entire state or several states if the wind is strong enough."

Ben stared at the schematics. "Do you think the man they took out of here is some type of nuclear scientist?"

"I can't imagine him being anything else," Jackson answered. "We need to take these, burn them, and then get that guy out of here."

Jackson started gathering the schematics before Ben could protest, and he reached for the colonel's arm, stopping him.

"Wait," Ben said. "Let's just think about this for a second."

"What is there to think about?" Jackson asked. "These people are building a nuke to blow a city off the face of the earth. They could be building multiple devices. I need to get this intelligence back to my commanding officers as quickly as possible. There is no higher priority than this."

"I agree with you that this is a top priority," Ben said. "But if we take all the stuff now, we're going to alert them to our presence. We need to take a minute and think about what we're trying to do. Because if we're caught, then nobody ever learns about what we found."

Jackson hesitated, and Ben could tell he didn't enjoy the prospect of waiting around. But the colonel wasn't an idiot. He recognized that coming up with a plan was better than flying by the seat-of-their-pants.

"What do you have in mind?" Jackson asked.

Ben knew that they didn't have time to wait for nightfall and the cover of darkness. For he knew Mark was already marching back to Asheville with more men to wipe them out.

Ben walked back to the front door, peered outside for a moment, and then closed the door. "This place isn't very big, right?"

"From what we saw, yeah," Jackson answered.

"That means they probably took that guy into one of the other trailers nearby," Ben replied. "If we can get him out of here without causing too much of a distraction, then we can come back to this trailer, grab all the schematics, then escape before they realize he's gone."

"Okay," Jackson said. "But what if we can't get him out?"

"Then we go with your plan," Ben answered. "We burn as much of this place as we can to the ground."

Jackson nodded and glanced back to the schematics on the desk. "No offense, but I hope we get to do my plan."

The moment word got out that food was missing, the entire camp was buzzing with concern. Liz had hoped her plan of searching every-thing all at once would mitigate some of the fallout, but it didn't do as much good as she had hoped.

The gathering crowd outside the main building where the food was stored was growing restless. Liz was still waiting to hear back from Nancy and Cole about their searches, but Liz and Sarah had found nothing.

"Who would take our food?" Shelby asked.

"And what happens if we don't get it back?" another asked.

The majority of the worry came from the women Nancy and Sarah had brought back from the clinic outside of Asheville. But some of Liz's closest friends were also expressing concern.

Susan and Kurt Johnson were standing outside, baby in their arms, and everyone felt the tension rising. "What about us? We were here before all of these people. That must count for something, right?"

"Oh, so you're more important than us?" one of the women from the clinic shouted back. "You think that just because you have a child that my life is worthless?"

"No one is saying that," Liz answered, and she felt her control over the situation slipping.

In total, there were twenty-nine people currently living at the facility. Over half of those people were from the women's clinic.

Just when the shouting was growing out of hand, Liz saw Cole and Nancy return from their searches. But the look on each of their faces didn't bode well for their situation.

"Everybody out here just needs to remain calm," Liz shouted. "I'm going to speak with the rest of my team and figure out what's going on. I just need all of you to be patient."

Liz turned her back to the grumbling crowd and joined Cole, Nancy, and Sarah inside the front doors of the mess hall. Once she was inside with everybody, she locked the door. She hoped that it was simply a precautionary measure, but it was one less thing for her to worry about.

"Tell me you found something good," Liz said.

Cole shook his head. "I couldn't find anything at the Johnsons or the Kippers."

"The tents the women from the clinic were using were all empty, too," Nancy said.

All of them looked to Liz to determine what they should do next, and Liz began to feel the weight of what needed to be done. She had grown tired over the past few weeks. With Ben busy with the exterior threats, Liz had been dealing with ones on the inside. And now it seemed that all of those tiny little grievances people had held in were all about to come out at once.

"Mom?" Sarah asked.

Liz nodded and pinched the bridge of her nose as she tried to concentrate. "If we don't have the food here and whoever took it won't come forth, then we need to figure out where they hid it. They probably buried it, and with that large amount of food they couldn't have gotten very far, so I want all of you to look for any churned-up dirt around the exterior of the fence."

"And if we don't find anything on the outside of the fence?" Nancy asked.

"We cross that bridge when we come to it," Liz answered. "All that matters is diffusing the situation. Is everyone here armed?"

Everyone nodded, and Liz saw that each of them had at least two firearms—a rifle and pistol. If push came to shove, then they could use intimidation to get their point across.

"Nancy, I want you up in the tower," Liz said. "Is

that something that you think you can handle?"

A shadow of a smile spread across Nancy's face, and she nodded. "No one will do anything stupid while I'm up there. I promise you that."

Liz had no doubt that Nancy could handle herself. She had come a long way from that first day of the EMP. She had become one of the best shots in the facility, almost as good as Ben.

"You don't take a shot unless it's absolutely necessary," Liz said. "Understand?"

Nancy nodded and then headed for the door. Once it was just Liz, Sarah, and Cole, she saw the crowd grow even more rambunctious outside.

"When you leave here, don't make any comments to anyone," Liz said. "If somebody presses you, just tell them that you're still looking for the food."

"What are you going to do once we're outside the fence?" Sarah asked.

Liz turned back toward the angry mob that was growing outside. "I'm going to try to make sure this doesn't turn ugly."

But before Liz could work her magic, somebody else had stepped up to the plate outside. And when Liz opened the door, she saw Jane Percy addressing the crowd.

"It seems to me that everybody here is innocent," Jane said, much to the crowd's delight. "And if no one here was responsible for the missing food, where's the only place we haven't checked?"

And as Jane turned around, Liz felt every eye the crowd bore into her soul. It was a silent penetrating gaze.

"I say we take a look inside the Rikers portable," Jane said.

Even before Liz could raise her voice, the crowd echoed in agreement. And there was only one reason for that woman to make such a statement.

They were going to find stolen food in their portable.

"All right, all right," Liz said, raising her arms high above her head, trying quite the swell of demands rising up from the crowd. "If that's going to make everybody calm down, then, of course, we can check our portable."

The crowd quieted down, and Liz turned her back to the crowd. She tried to rack her brain of how she would explain what they found in her portable. There would be an incredible amount of anger and betrayal, but Liz decided to get out in front of it before things became worse.

"I'm sorry," Liz said again, holding up her hand and turning around to face the crowd. "I do have a confession to make."

The crowd whispered amongst themselves, and out of the corner of her eye, Liz saw Jane begin to frown.

"I don't think it's a secret that the mood around the facility has been one of frustration lately," Liz said.

"And in an effort to combat that, I decided to run a drill."

The whispers shifted to confusion.

"I thought I could bring us together by presenting a challenge to all of us," Liz said. "But seeing as how much more frustration this has caused, I can see it was a bad idea."

"What are you talking about?" Shelby asked.

"The food is perfectly safe," Liz answered, and she watched as relief rippled through the crowd. "I stored it in our portable."

"Why would you do that?" Susan asked.

Liz raised her voice, and the members quieted down. "There is going to be adversity for us in the future. And if we can't rise to the challenge during a crisis, then we don't have a shot in hell of fighting the real thing. And I wanted to show all of us that we can't blame and point fingers about who might've taken what. We need to be a united front."

Liz saw that she had struck a chord as the crowd glanced at one another. Liz then turned to Jane, who was glowering at her.

"I think today was a perfect example of learning to trust," Liz said. "Because without trust, there can be no foundation, and without a strong foundation, our community will fall apart."

Despite the odds and the Hail Mary longshot Liz had thrown, somehow, people were buying into what she was saying. She hoped that people would simply be so relieved that the food wasn't missing that they would be more open to forgiving a small misunderstanding.

It turned out she was right.

But there was at least one person in the crowd who wasn't excited about the news. And Jane Percy decided to capitalize on the moment before she lost all of her momenta.

"I think that was a terrible exercise to run," Jane said. "You had the entire community up in arms. I'm not sure that's the kind of leadership I want to see around here."

And with that one phrase, Liz finally understood what Jane was up to. She was trying to get the community to turn against them so they could step in and start running things. It was a clever plan, but Jane had underestimated Liz.

"Ben and I never said that we were the sole people in charge," Liz said. "Everybody who stays here plays an active role in our survival. The only way that any of this works is if we all work together."

"I completely agree," Jane said. "But it seems to me, the balance of power in this community is centered around you and your family." She turned around and faced the crowd. "The Rikers have all the keys to every resource in the community, and they control the one commodity that all of us can't live without. They have the weapons, they have nice accommodations, and they make all the schedules. Don't you think it's time we all have a bigger say in how this place is run?"

The crowd returned to Jane's side, and Liz suddenly found herself in a political battle. She had no intention of losing this place, but she also had no intention of becoming a dictator. The moment she started waving her gun around, she would lose that trust she had spoken so highly of moments before.

"I think everybody having a more active say is more than fair," Liz said. "So why don't we put it to a vote?" Liz stepped forward, choosing to go all-in against Jane here and now. "This evening, we will have a meeting in the mess hall, and everybody in the community will speak their peace about who they think should be running this place."

Liz turned to Jane, waiting to see if she had any type of rebuke. When Jane nodded, Liz knew that they had a lot of work ahead of them. But first and foremost was getting the food out of her portable and back into the mess hall.

*B*en and Jackson hung back in the woods for another twenty minutes, watching the trailer where they believed the scientist had been taken. He was on the edge of the trailer park, which would at least make it easy to get in and out quickly; whether or not they would do that without raising the alarm remained to be seen.

"What do you think they're doing to him in there?" Ben asked.

Jackson shook his head. "I'm sure they're not sitting around and singing 'Kumbaya.'" He raised the small pair of binoculars he brought with him. "Those newspapers were a good idea. I can't see a damn thing." He lowered the binoculars. "What I wouldn't give for some heat vision goggles right about now."

"Nothing like doing things analog," Ben said. "You ready to go over the plan one more time?"

Jackson nodded. "I go in first, and then you follow, clearing my left side. We take them quickly and without firearms, if possible. From there, we bound and gag our scientist so he doesn't make a fuss and then retreat toward the trailer with the schematics to gather the intelligence. Then we toss this baby into the portable on our way out." He raised his hand, holding a large grenade. "Boom."

With the plan in place, all they had to do now was execute it. Easier said than done.

"Let's get into position," Ben said.

The pair moved stealthily through the woods remaining out of sight from the guards who were still circling the perimeter. They knew the moment anybody raised the alarm, all hell would break loose. And despite their plan, there was no guarantee of success.

From what reconnaissance they managed to obtain, they saw no guards posted outside the trailer where they believed the scientist was taken. But they knew there were still at least two men inside. Nobody had come in or out since the scientist was brought in.

They waited a few more minutes for the next round of guards to pass the backside of the trailer's perimeter, and once they were clear, Jackson nodded for them to proceed.

They approached the door, silent as the night, but Ben could have sworn that his heart was hammering so loud that it was going to give away their position. But he kept his composure, knowing that any wrong move could be his last, and with so much at stake, there was no room for error.

Jackson held up his hand and counted down from five. Once he reached zero and formed a fist, he quickly opened the door, and their plan was thrust into action.

The moment the door was open, they caught the attention of the two guards inside. They only waited a few seconds before they reached for their weapons, but it was enough time for Ben and Jackson to have the jump on them. The priority was subduing them but also making sure that they didn't raise any alarms.

Ben clamped his hand over one of the men's mouths and muffled his throaty scream as he plunged the knife between the ribs on his left side. The Kevlar he wore didn't fully wrap all the way around, so it allowed him to penetrate the armor from the side.

The position of the blade should have penetrated his heart, but Ben had aimed too low. He was forced to remove the blade and then shoved the bloodied tip of his knife into the man's armpit. Here, a cluster of veins and arteries were located, and it was a quick place to cause the man to bleed out.

Ben had never stabbed another person before, and the resistance of the muscle, bone, and tendon of the human body was both formidable and sickening. The man continued to struggle even after the blood ran out of him, smacking Ben with his waning strength until the very last drop had vanished from him, and there was nothing left, and he collapsed to the floor.

Ben drew in a sharp breath, not even realizing he'd been holding it, and when he looked up and saw the second man at Jackson's feet, he realized that they had done it.

"Ben," Jackson said, whispering harshly, "help me with him."

Ben was still in a bit of a daze, but he realized that the scientist was bound to a chair against the wall. He was now shirtless, and his body was covered in red welts and bruises. He looked disoriented, and Ben figured the man had been tortured while he was inside.

Ben helped remove the scientist's restraints and then put his left arm over his shoulders, and Jackson did the same on the right. They lifted him up and dragged him toward the door. Jackson opened the door and peered outside, making sure that nobody else heard the commotion.

"I think we're in the clear." Jackson turned back to the scientist and slapped the side of his face trying to wake him up. "Hey, buddy, are you still with us?"

The scientist grumbled something, but the way he swayed his head back and forth made it look like he was drunk.

Jackson shook his head. "Looks like we'll have to carry him most of the way. Do you think you can do that?"

Ben nodded. "The plan stays the same. We still need to hit that other trailer with the plans on the way back."

Jackson adjusted the scientist on his shoulder. He shook his head. "I don't know if we'll be able to carry all that stuff and him. We might have to go ahead and torch the place."

"No torch," the scientist muttered quietly to himself. "There are other people here."

Jackson and Ben exchanged a quick glance.

"How many other people?" Jackson asked.

The scientist took a few deep breaths and finally managed to lift his head. He started to regain some of his strength and was able to stand up somewhat on his own. "There are other engineers here. People held against their will, like me."

Voices could be heard through the thin trailer walls. The guards were once again on the backside of the trailer park, making the rounds. Jackson covered the scientist's mouth to keep him quiet, and Ben found himself holding his breath.

The sound of the guard's voices sounded like they were outside forever. But when they finally faded from earshot, Ben exhaled.

"If you don't get them out now, they will be killed," the scientist said.

Ben remembered the photographs they had found in one of the trailers and how the images were of men and women found naked and bound. He figured those people could've been family members or other scientists and engineers who refused to do the work.

"We'll come back for them later," Jackson said.

The scientist shook his head, adamant about his requests. "I'm not going to leave them behind."

Jackson groaned and then let Ben hold up the scientist while he retrieved the chair the man had been sitting. He pulled the chair up behind him, and they sat the scientist back down.

"If we're going to help your friends, you need to help us," Jackson said. "How many total guards are at this camp?"

The scientist grimaced as if the mere act of thinking made his body light up with pain. "Twelve."

"So we've already taken out two guys," Ben said.

"Yes, I can count," Jackson said. "Do they have any communication with other camps? Radios, that kind of thing?"

The scientist nodded. "There is a radio in the trailer at the center of camp."

Ben looked at Jackson. "Right where we saw all of those guards go when they were off duty."

"The radio will be too difficult to get to if that's the case," Jackson said, and then he glanced at the grenade in his hand and then looked to Ben.

"We'd give away our position," Ben said. "Not to mention we wouldn't kill all of them. For all we know, there could only be one or two guys in that trailer, and then we alert the rest of them when the grenade explodes."

Jackson gave it some thought while the scientist hunched forward and cradled his head in his hands. Ben was already mentally calculating the number of trailers spread out over the park. Though the lot was small, it was still a significant amount of space, and recovering all of the scientist's colleagues without raising an alarm would be next to impossible.

"Please," the scientist said, almost as if he could read their minds and how both men were leaning toward just leaving with what they came for. "They have families. They are good people."

"We have families," Jackson said. "We're good people. We can't save everybody in this fight."

"I know that," the scientist said. "And I'm not asking you to save everybody. I'm just asking you to save the people here." He looked up at Jackson. "Is that so much to ask?"

"It's not that we don't want to," Jackson answered. "But you are the most vital asset. We need to get you out of here as quickly as possible."

"They can always find someone else to do my work," the scientist answered. "And if it's weapons that you're trying to prevent from being built, every engineer and scientist at this location is tasked with making weapons. Weapons used to kill the military and any civilians who resist them."

It was a smart play by scientists because Ben saw

the colonel consider changing his response.

"What kind of weapons?" Jackson asked.

"The main goal of every scientist in this camp is to get the heavy machinery operating again," the scientist said. "Humvees, tanks, helicopters, rockets, anything that could do real damage to the military and the people's needs."

"There weren't any of those things in this camp," Ben said. "Where are they being stored?"

"In the town," the scientist said. "They only bring the components fried by the EMP, so the entire vehicle doesn't need to be kept here. They have vehicles stashed all around the country, just waiting for the parts to be finished in places like these."

"They told you about the EMP?" Jackson asked.

"I've seen what happened," the scientist answered. "They didn't need to tell me what happened for me to have figured it out on my own."

The voices appeared again as the guards made another lap around the trailer park. All it would take would be for one of them to knock on this door, and everything they were talking about would be moot.

"We're running out of time either way," Ben said, and then he glanced down to the scientist. "Are you going to cause trouble for us if we don't rescue your friends?"

"Look at me," the scientist answered. "Do I look like I'm in the condition to cause any trouble?"

The guard's voices on patrol again faded, and Ben

knew this was their window to escape. "What do you want to do?"

The longer Jackson took to deliberate, the more Ben was convinced that they would help the scientist's friends.

"Do you have any details of what is specifically in each of these trailers?" Jackson asked.

The scientist nodded. "They keep all of us in the same trailer at night to sleep. We talk amongst ourselves before bed. The hours we keep are grueling, but we have managed to keep somewhat of a comradery."

Jackson proceeded to pry information from the scientist to confirm what they could about the contents of each trailer. Most trailers had at least one guard stationed though the scientist was the exception because he was working on the biggest project: the nuke.

One guard was much more manageable than two and could potentially flip the odds in their favor. But they would still need to be careful about raising the alarm because, again, any wrong move could be their last.

"If we do this, it's going to be faster if we don't have you with us," Jackson said. "We'll get you into the woods and keep you there until we have everyone. That will also give us a rallying point to get to if things turn south."

"Thank you," the scientist said. "Thank you for

doing this."

Ben didn't think he had ever seen somebody so exhausted. He watched as the scientist deflated in his chair, and for a moment, Ben thought the man was going to pass out. But he managed to actually stand on his own two feet.

"I can make it there on my own steam," the scientist said.

Ben and Jackson didn't object, but they kept the man between them as they hurried back toward the woods. They positioned the scientist as close to the horses as they could get without being gone for too long. Time was already against them.

With the scientist secure, Jackson returned to the perimeter of the trailer park. From what they could tell, no alarms were raised and the guards at the camp suspected nothing.

"It makes sense to start on the outside and work our way inward," Jackson said.

Ben agreed. "We can start there." He pointed to the nearest trailer that they were certain had people in it. "Ready?"

Jackson nodded. "Let's go."

The pair emerged from the woods. They moved swiftly toward the first trailer, and they kept the same formation as they had for the other entries. This time, when Jackson opened the door, he had to take on the person on the other side all by himself, but Ben moved in to help keep the man quiet.

But before the guard was dead, the scientist or engineer they had stashed away inside made a break for the door. Ben lunged forward, and he ended up tackling the man to the floor.

The prisoner's instincts were to fight back immediately, and it took all of Ben's strength to keep him from escaping.

"We're here to help," Ben said. "We're not going to hurt you."

The engineer looked from Ben over to Jackson just as the guard gurgled his last breath of life. It sounded like a painful death.

The engineer stopped squirming and finally settled down, allowing Ben to lift him up just as Jackson removed the blade from the dead man's belly.

"Who are you?" the man asked, cowering as he stared at the blood dripping from Jackson's knife.

"We'll explain later," Ben answered. "But we don't have a lot of time." He stepped toward the man to grab his arm, but the engineer retreated out of reach. "We need to leave."

"They'll kill us if we leave," the engineer said. "They've already killed so many." The man was horrified.

Ben remembered the trailer with all of the photographs on the wall and wondered if this man had known any of them. The guards here probably used the photographs as threats, visuals to keep the rest of their prisoners in line.

"We know," Ben said. "But if we don't leave now, they're going to kill more people."

The engineer considered this as Jackson waited by the door, listening for any movement outside. Finally, he nodded and then walked over to Jackson. But before Ben stepped outside, he caught a quick glance at the drawings on the table. They were crude flying apparatuses, things that looked like they would have been advanced over one hundred years ago. Ben frowned, unsure of how these weapons would be a threat to the military, but he grabbed one and stuffed it into his pocket.

Ben and Jackson returned to the section of the woods where they had left the nuclear scientist and then returned to gather the others.

For the next three trailers, everything went smoothly. No one suspected their entrance, and both Jackson and Ben remained efficient in recovering the other engineers. But when they neared the fourth trailer, they encountered their first problem.

The guards circling the perimeter decided to take an early break and cut through the center of the trailer park, crossing paths with Ben and Jackson. Both parties froze, neither moving as they all waited for the other person to make a move.

Thankfully, Jackson had made the first move, and once the gunfire started, Ben jumped into action.

The trio sped toward the tree line, Ben holding the grenade in his hand, ready to blow the trailer where the nuclear scientist had been working, but then stopped. What was inside was valuable not just to The New Order but to anyone fighting them.

"Ben, let's go!" Jackson shouted, leading the other engineer to the forest line where they would meet the others.

Ben didn't hesitate. He pocketed the grenade and then rushed into the portable. It was still empty, all of the schematics and sheets of paper that had been strung up. He grabbed as many of the sheets of paper as he could find, not bother looking at what he was grabbing because he knew he wouldn't be able to understand it anyway.

One of the guards banged against the door, and Ben shot at him, buying him a few moments. Out of time, Ben shot out the window and leaped through the glass. He landed awkwardly on the ground outside, but he had no idea how much of the glass had scratched him. He chucked the grenade back behind him, into the shattered window, and then made it into the woods before it exploded.

Ben's adrenaline was amped, and he was so wired from the fight that he didn't see Jackson and the others until they were halfway to the horses.

Once they all reached the animals, Ben knew that they didn't have enough horses to carry everybody. And as Jackson hoisted the nuclear scientist onto the back of the animal, the others scrambled to get up.

"What about us?" a man asked.

"Just keep running, and we'll hold them off as long as we can," Jackson answered.

Jackson fired back at the enemy who was chasing them into the woods. Ben reached his horse, where two others were clamoring to get on the animal. The horse bucked and reared, stress from all of the frantic energy surrounding it. These animals weren't used to such excitement.

"Let her go," Ben yelled, motioning for the people to get away from the horse before it hurt itself.

The escaped engineers and scientists were stuck between being kicked by the horse and shot in the back, and Ben saw the wild fear in everyone's eyes.

Ben tried to calm the horse down, but the gunfire grew louder and closer as the enemy advanced through the woods.

Ben looked to Jackson, who was still mounted on the horse with the nuclear scientist. As he made his way over, the colonel was barely able to keep control of the animal.

"I'm going to take the scientist farther down the road and come back for people," Jackson said. "You think you can stay here and hold the ground?"

Ben looked to the other prisoners who were frazzled from the fight. He nodded. "Just make it fast."

Jackson turned the animal around and kicked its belly, sending it flying through the woods.

Ben had a spare pistol, and he reloaded. "Who here knows how to shoot?"

The three scientists and engineers who had followed Ben remained skittish, and they kept their eyes peeled on the danger that was heading right for them.

"Hey!" Ben shouted, pulling their attention away from the enemy advancing toward him. "I can't hold them off all on my own. Have any of you handled a weapon before?"

Finally, one of the scientists stepped forward. He nodded shakily and extended his hand for the weapon. "I know how to shoot a little bit."

Ben handed the pistol over to the man. "What's your name?"

"Daniel," he answered.

"Daniel, I need you to go ten feet that way and make sure no one flanks us from your side," Ben answered, shoving Daniel in the direction he needed him to go. "You hang out by that big tree there, and you don't move, and you shoot anything that comes your way." He reached for a few spare magazines and tossed them to Daniel. "You know how to reload?"

Daniel nodded and then ducked from the gunfire.

"Good, now go!" Ben shouted.

Daniel sprinted over to the tree and crouched down behind it for cover. Ben wasn't sure how good of a shot he was, but so long as he kept firing, it would at least buy them a little time.

"Why can't we just keep running?" the other engineer asked. "Aren't we just sitting ducks here?"

"If we keep running, they keep chasing," Ben answered. "But if we hold our ground, it will slow them down, hopefully, long enough that you can get to safety when Jackson comes back."

A bullet whizzed by, and Ben pressed himself back up against a tree while the others ducked.

"Just stay down and don't make yourself a big target," Ben said.

When Jackson returned, the gunfire between Ben and the encroaching enemy had intensified, but from what Ben could see, the enemy had slowed their advance. Jackson picked up the next scientist and took off.

The enemy had dug their heels in as well, and each time Ben peered around the edge of the tree to take a shot, he never had an opening.

By the time Jackson came back for the last man, the enemy had only advanced a few more feet, but they knew that once the last scientist was gone and Ben was by himself that the enemy would grow bolder. But what he found interesting was the fact that none of the enemy fighters brought any of the more advanced weapons the engineers had been working on. Ben thought that was a good sign, signaling that perhaps the scientists hadn't finished the work they were brought here to perform.

"Last one!" Jackson shouted.

"I'll be right behind you," Ben said.

Jackson nodded and turned the animal, but another

barrage of gunfire spooked the beast, and he reared on its hind legs, causing Daniel to fall to the ground. There was a snapping sound and then a scream, and Ben knew what had happened before he saw Daniel's broken leg.

Jackson quickly dismounted the horse and rushed over to Daniel. The bone was coming through the cloth of the pants, and the man was wincing in pain from the compound fracture.

"We can't move him," Jackson said.

"No," Daniel said. "Don't leave me here."

"A bullet would be kinder than just leaving him here," Jackson said, and then he brandished his weapon.

"No!" Daniel shouted. "Please, don't do this."

Ben glanced behind him and saw the enemy moving closer. It was only a matter of time before they were overrun and then everybody would be at risk. But Ben wasn't in the mood to lose anybody in this fight right now.

"Listen to me," Ben said, looking at Daniel. "If we move you, we run the risk of doing a lot more damage. Even if we save your life, it might cripple your leg to the point where we have to amputate, and you may not even survive that."

Daniel's face was dripping with sweat; his eyes were so big that Ben could see the red veins bulging. "I don't want to die. Not here. Not now. Move me."

Ben looked to Jackson, who still had his pistol out and at the ready, but then finally put it away.

"You're going to have to help me get him on the horse," Jackson said. "And we need to keep his leg stabilized as much as possible."

Jackson sidled up on the left while Ben took the right, keeping the bulk of his attention on the leg itself. "We lift on three, ready? One, two, three."

Ben and Jackson lifted in unison, and the moment Daniel was off the ground, the man screamed in agony. Knowing that if they stopped, it would only make things worse for Daniel. The man thrashed, making it difficult to carry him and only causing more pain.

"Keep still!" Jackson shouted.

They eventually heaved him onto the horse's back, and the shock was so great that Daniel passed out. Jackson mounted the animal and kept Daniel from sliding off. "I stashed everyone down by a rock outcropping. From there, we should have an even better cover so long as we get to the ridge. Once we have the high ground, they should back off."

Ben nodded. "I'll meet you there."

Jackson kicked the animal and then raced off. Alone, now, Ben fired off two more shots before he retreated to his own horse.

Once Ben was on his horse and out of the bulk of the gunfire, he felt himself relax a little bit, his mind regaining clarity and he started to think about what came next.

Jackson's idea of heading to the ridge was a good one, but he wasn't sure what the endgame plan was? Were those fighters going to chase them all the way back to Asheville?

Ben was still frantic to escape when he caught up with Jackson and the others and then saw the colonel had dismounted by the rocks and was in no hurry to keep moving.

"What are you doing?" Ben asked, keeping on the horse. "They were following me. Even on foot, it won't take them very long—"

"They won't follow us," Jackson answered.

Ben frowned. "Why not?"

Jackson said nothing and looked back to the nuclear scientists gathered around Daniel as they examined his broken leg.

"Because they already have what they want," Jackson answered. "Isn't that right, doctor?"

The nuclear scientist looked up from Daniel and then saw the blood on the doctor's hands. He had been trying to set the bone, but when Ben saw one of the engineers close Daniel's eyes, he knew the man was already gone.

"The device they brought me in to create is already finished." The scientist stared down at the blood on his hands. "I finished it earlier today before you came to get me. They were going to kill me. They were simply arguing about how to do it."

Ben glanced behind them and then listened for any

shouts or gunfire in the woods. But the force had gone silent. They weren't following.

Jackson removed his sidearm and aimed the pistol at the scientist. "Son of a bitch lied to us. Just to save his own skin."

The scientist showed no sign of fear and simply stared the weapon down. "I have been living under the threat of violence for the past several weeks. Do you really think that you're going to intimidate me by shoving a gun in my face?"

"How about if I pull the trigger?" Jackson asked.

Ben dismounted and walked over to diffuse the situation. "Everybody needs to calm down."

Jackson snarled. "This bastard made a device for a group of terrorists that could blow up a major city and have devastating effects for our efforts to turn the tide of this fight."

"And if you kill me, you won't know where they're sending it," the scientist said.

Jackson didn't lower his weapon, but he definitely looked more intrigued now. "Bullshit."

Ben turned to the scientist. "Do you really know where they're going with it?"

"I don't know what they plan to do once the pieces are put together, but I know where my piece went," the scientist answered.

"Well," Ben said. "We're all ears."

"I heard them talking about a city north of here," the scientist said. "Johnson something."

"Johnson City?" Ben asked.

"Yeah, I think that's it," the scientist answered.

Ben and Jackson exchanged a glance. That city was one of the possible intelligence reports of where the enemy had been gathering.

"When did they leave with the item?" Jackson asked.

"Someone came and picked it up about an hour before you showed up," he answered.

"Did they have transportation?" Ben asked.

The scientist shook his head. "Not that I saw, but he might have."

Ben walked over to Jackson, the pair moving away from the rest of the group to speak in private.

"If we assume that they were on foot, we could theoretically catch up with them on horses," Ben said.

"And if they had one of these vehicles working, then they would probably already be in Johnson City," Jackson replied.

"We came all this way to stop these people from obtaining a nuclear weapon," Ben said. "If we turn back now, we'll be coming home empty-handed."

Jackson considered this a moment and then nodded. "I'll go. You take the rest of the scientists back to Asheville." He headed for his horse, and Ben rushed forward to try to stop him.

"You can't go in alone. You don't even know what you're facing," Ben said.

"I joined the military to be able to handle myself

during these types of situations," Jackson said. "I'll be fine."

"I'm not sure about that," the scientist said.

Jackson paused before he could mount his horse. He turned around and glared at the scientist. "That a threat?"

"He's right," Ben said. "Johnson City is their main hub, and a mission this important, carrying a component of a nuclear device, I'm sure they will be well guarded. You track them alone and there's no guarantee that you'll come back. You're going to need help in order to get through this."

Jackson gestured to the men and women they had saved. "And what about them? We can't take them all with us; they'll slow us down."

"Leave us," the scientist said. "It's clear the enemy doesn't want us anymore, or they would have kept chasing. They have other orders to follow."

Ben walked over to the scientist and then handed him some of his rations. "These should last you long enough to get to Asheville."

"And what's in Asheville?" the scientist asked.

"Help," Ben answered. "You go there and tell the military personnel that you were with Colonel Jackson, and you tell them what you told us."

Jackson walked over, removed his patch from his shoulder with a knife, and slammed it down in the scientist's hand. "Show them that. It'll help give you some credibility."

Ben also handed over the schematics and drawings he managed to steal from the portable before he blew it up. "These should help as well," Ben said. "Just make sure you get back alive."

The scientist stared at all of the documentation in his hands. He looked back to the others that have been imprisoned with him. "I'm not sure all of them will follow me. Some of them might try to go home. I'm sure not all of their families are dead."

"What about your family?" Ben asked.

The scientist shook his head. "I don't have any family. Not anymore."

"Why did you still build it for them then?" Jackson asked.

The scientist stared at the blood of his hands, unable to look away. He seemed fascinated by the sight of it. "Because I am a coward who wants to live." He looked up. "I just need to figure out why."

Ben could see that this man was struggling to find a purpose. He had been there himself several times throughout his life. "What's most important right now is getting back to Asheville. The easy part is over. Now comes the difficult part of trying to come to terms with what you did."

The scientist nodded and then joined the other engineers. Ben walked over to his horse and mounted the animal. Jackson did the same.

On their way out, Ben turned back around to look

at the people they'd rescued. "They should bury Daniel."

Jackson kept his attention forward. "I doubt they will. They're scientists. They're not religious people."

Ben thought that was an oversimplification of a much broader issue. "Sometimes people can surprise you."

"I hope not," Jackson said.

Ben was quiet for a moment, letting the colonel's words marinate.

"That thing you said about the hard part the scientist had coming, it reminded me of something my father used to tell me," Jackson said.

"Yeah? What was that?" Ben asked.

"He told me that there is always an easy part, and a hard part, in everything you do in life," Jackson answered. "We don't always get to pick which part comes first, but we do most of the time. He said life is all about the choices we make, and we can choose to take the hard part first and then have an easy time later or be a slacker and take the easy part first and the hard part later. I always liked to take the hard part earlier myself."

Ben nodded. "Same." He gestured to the camp where they had just come. "Do you think that was the easy part we had earlier or the hard part?"

"I'm hoping it was the hard part," Jackson answered. "But something tells me that I'm not going to get my wish."

illie had always been an opportunist. And after witnessing the debacle with the food situation, he sensed an opening to better his position at the facility.

Willie was used to being top dog, but he recognized that he wasn't the big man on campus here, not something he enjoyed. But in order to change his position, he needed to determine where to place his loyalties.

The moment he met the Riker family, Willie immediately disliked them. And it wasn't just because of their daughter and her little friend. They had an arrogance about them that he didn't appreciate. He had been around those kinds of people his entire life, and they always looked down on him.

But after hearing Jane speak, Willie realized that the Percy family was a group he could get behind. It was clear to him that the Rikers had not planned any type of drill to see how the community would react to their missing food but instead came up with an excuse on the fly of why the food was there in the first place.

The Rikers also wouldn't try to steal food and hoard for themselves. They were too self-righteous to try something like that, which meant someone had taken the food and planted it on them in hopes of sewing distrust against them.

Rumblings around the camp and little whispers allowed Willie to put together the story of a feud between the Percy family and the Riker family that stretched back for years. And if the Percy's didn't like the Rikers, Willie thought he might get along with them just dandy.

Willie knocked on the Percy's portable and stepped back, waiting for an answer. When the door finally opened, he saw the husband, Lester.

"What the hell do you want?" Lester asked.

Willie offered a friendly smile and extended his hand. "Mr. Percy, it's nice to finally meet you in person."

Lester stared down at the hand but didn't shake it. He looked back up at Willie. "That doesn't answer my question."

Willie lowered his hand and laughed. "Sorry about that. My name is Willie Smith. I was part of the group that came in a few weeks ago."

Lester stood his ground. "From the women's clinic?"

Willie nodded. "That's right. My girlfriend and I were at the clinic when the power went out."

Lester gave Willie a good look up and down and crossed his arms. "You're the one who was knocking around that girl, weren't you?"

Willie had been confronted by other men about his abuse before, and it was always a touchy subject. There were fewer and fewer men who believed a man had the right to hit his woman when they were getting out of line. It was a disgrace.

"Knocking around is subjective," Willie said.

"Not these days." The voice came from inside the portable, and Lester stepped aside, and Jane Percy came into view. "Especially not in this house."

Willie smiled and nodded. "Of course. It's nice to meet you, ma'am." Again he extended his hand, but Jane also declined.

"What the hell do you want, Willie?" Jane asked.

Willie noted the twang in the voice, but these weren't a stupid pair of hillbillies who had crawled out from beneath a rock. These were people were organized, motivated, and smart. If he wanted to join the winning side, then he needed to convince them that he was an asset.

"I've come to offer my services to you," Willie said.

"And what exactly do you think we need help with?" Jane asked.

"I know that the food mishap wasn't a planned

drill," Willie answered. "And I think you and your family had something to do with all of that."

Jane was quiet, and Willie could tell that she was weighing her options. "That's quite a bold statement from someone in your position."

Despite what people might have said about Willie, the man had an uncanny ability to read people. It was one of the reasons, really the only reason, he had survived so long in this world. He knew how to pick his mark. It was why he had chosen to date Carolina. He knew she was someone who would keep her mouth shut, someone who understood what it meant to be controlled.

And from what he could read of Jane Percy, he could tell this was a woman who had been underestimated her entire life and probably looked over by many men. And despite how often people talk about not caring about what other people think, in Willie's experience, everyone, especially women, cared about what other people thought. It was coded in the human genome. It was why we were such social creatures. We wanted to be accepted.

Willie thought he might be able to flirt his way to get Jane on his side. "Someone in my position is in a unique spot to recognize an opportunity. And I see opportunity with you." He flashed his award-winning grin. It worked most of the time.

Jane smiled and leaned a little closer. She lowered her voice to a whisper to where only Willie could hear.

"And what exactly do you think that opportunity will be?"

Willie smiled even wider. He knew he had her hook, line, and sinker. "I think that's for you to decide." He could tell that Jane was eating it up, and when she laughed, he mirrored the same reaction. But before he could enjoy his victory lap, Jane grabbed Willie's arm and spun him around, pinning his arm behind his back. "What the hell are you doing?"

"You listen to me very carefully," Jane answered. "You don't know a damned thing about me, or my family, or what we want. And if I see you come sniffing around here again, I promise you that you won't be able to crawl away after I'm done with you."

Jane shoved Willie forward, and he stumbled down the steps from the portable. He rubbed the arm Jane had pinned and glanced up at Jane, staring down at him with Lester grinning.

"And if I see you touch that woman again, I will put a bullet in you myself," Jane said. "Got it, asshole?" She didn't wait for a response and returned inside the portable with Lester giving him one more death stare before going inside himself.

Willie felt his cheeks turn red with embarrassment. He hated being played like a fool. And he hated it even more when it was done by a woman.

Anger building up inside of him, Willie stormed off. He reached into his pocket for the pack of cigarettes he had and was so upset that he dropped the carton to the ground. "Fucking hell." He snatched the carton off the grass and then bit one of the cigarette tips between his teeth as he pulled it out. He struggled to click the lighter, and after a half-dozen misses, he threw both the cigarette and the lighter to the ground.

"Fucking bitch," Willie said, muttering to himself as he stewed in his own anger. "I went there to help them, and they throw that goodwill in my face."

Willie felt his anger rising. He was able to keep it at bay most of the time. He had actually gone to therapy at one point to try to cure himself. It had come after roughing up a woman real bad, and when he saw the aftermath once he cooled off, he realized that maybe he did need help.

The therapy helped at first. He believed he could find ways to help channel his rage and stop it before it grew out of control. It really wasn't about curing, he learned, but more about managing his symptoms. He had experienced his own trauma growing up at the hands of his father. All he had known his entire child-hood was abusive hands, and he carried that legacy with him as an adult.

But after a few weeks of going to the sessions, Willie was starting to become frustrated. No matter how much he tried to keep his anger in check, there was nothing that stopped it from bubbling up. And the fact that he was now trying to stop it only made the anger worse. Eventually, all that anger came out one night when his girlfriend didn't make dinner the way he normally liked it.

It was the only time in any of Willie's relationships where the police were called and he was arrested. He lost control and had done prison time because of it. He was sent to counseling in prison as well to help deal with his anger management, but it was the same story inside. No matter how much therapy he received, the anger never went away.

And if he were completely honest with himself, which he never really was in therapy, he enjoyed the anger. He liked it when he finally let go and did what he wanted. He never felt more powerful than when he was unleashing that anger on something so fragile. He didn't know why that made him feel good, but it did.

And right now, he wanted to feel good.

Willie made a beeline for the tents. They were terrible flimsy things, and he hadn't had a good night's sleep since they had arrived there. Sleeping on the ground wasn't doing any favors for his back. He spied their tent and ripped open the flap, finding Carolina inside reading a book she had brought with them from the clinic. They had a small library there, and she was always reading, her nose in those stupid books. He never understood it.

"We need to go," Willie said.

Carolina immediately perked up to attention. "What's wrong?"

Willie grabbed hold of her arm and squeezed hard

enough to cause her to flinch. "It doesn't matter what's wrong. What matters is that I need you to do what I say when I say it!" He barred his teeth as he pulled her closer. When she cowered from his touch and his proximity, he felt a rush of excitement course through him. She was afraid of him because he was stronger than her, and that was what he enjoyed the most.

But then Willie saw a flash of defiance appear on her face. That elation of power was replaced with his own twinge of fear.

"No," Carolina said.

"What?" Willie asked.

Carolina pulled her arm free, and she rose to her knees. "I don't have to go with you, and I don't have to do what you say. I'm staying here."

Willie shoved his finger in her face. "You are coming with me, now."

Carolina shook her head, remaining defiant. "No."

In all the time that the pair had been dating, Carolina had never stood up to him, and the fact that she was making her stand now only added more fuel to the anger burning inside of Willie.

"You think that you're safe here?" Wille asked. "You think that these people are going to keep you around? You're worthless and pathetic!" He struggled to keep his voice down, not wanting to draw attention to himself.

"I am not useless," Carolina said, though her meek

tone betrayed the confidence of the words. "I'm going to help build houses for the other women."

Willie laughed, and his reaction was almost as bad as a slap to her face. "You think that you have friends here? You think that they're going to keep you around after they find out you can't do anything? How are you going to build a house, Carolina? You can't even take care of yourself." He leaned closer, almost hissing now. "I'm the only one who can help you."

He saw the conflict on her face. Part of her believed him, but there was another part that believed in herself. Willie thought he had broken that part of her, but apparently, it had been repaired.

"This isn't a discussion," Willie said, grabbing Carolyn's arm again. "We are leaving, and we are leaving now."

Willie yanked Carolina out of the tent and immediately headed for the exit. He was so blinded by his own anger he was oblivious to what they would do once they were gone. There wasn't anything left in this area, which meant they would have to find a new town. A new place to start over.

Carolina defied him the entire way, struggling and pulling, silently causing a scene. "Let me go. I don't want to go with you."

"You'll go wherever I damn well say," Willie said.

Willie was so focused on getting to the gate that he didn't see the look of determination on Carolina's face.

He had left himself vulnerable for an attack that he never believed Carolina was capable of giving.

"I said no!" Carolina lunged forward, reaching up with her nails, and clawed at the side of Willie's face. She pressed down hard and cut his cheek, drawing blood.

"Gah!" Willie released her and immediately reached for his cheek. He looked back at her in disbelief and saw she was in the same state of shock.

It was the perfect opportunity for her to make a run for it, but she was paralyzed by her own action. And that was her mistake.

"You fucking bitch!" Willie lunged forward and grabbed her by the neck. He squeezed hard enough to choke her and then lifted her high enough to where her feet kicked and dangled. "Who the fuck do you think you are?"

Carolina held onto Willie's arms for dear life, and her lips started to turn blue.

"You touch me like that? Me?" Willie squeezed harder and then shook her like a rag doll. He had never felt this strong before, never this powerful, and the harder he squeezed, the more life he saw drain from her eyes, the more excited he became.

This was who he truly was. This was the person he was meant to be, not somebody who hid behind conventional social norms. He was too good for that now, and he hated that he had wasted so much time, trying to pretend to be something he wasn't.

Just when he thought the light was going to fade from Carolina's eyes, Willie watched as a final burst of strength erupted from Carolina, much like the final spasm in a body after it dies and the brain is still sending electrical signals through the muscles.

Carolina struck Willie in the groin, and both of them crumpled to the ground, with Willie groaning in pain and Carolina drawing raspy gasps of breath.

Willie rolled to his side in just enough time to watch Carolina stumble to her hands and feet and then crawl back toward the main building.

"You bitch! You fucking bitch!" Willie wanted nothing more at that moment than to kill her. But the pain radiating through his body didn't cooperate with the demands from his mind.

Willie gagged a few times and then vomited; the pain was so intense. The hot bile dripped from his lips, burning his throat and tongue. He spat, unable able to get the taste of puke from his mouth, and eventually managed to stand up on his own two feet.

But when he rose, he saw that other women had emerged from the tents and had seen what he had done and, more importantly, what Carolina had done.

The act of defiance from one of their own seemed to have triggered a level of courage in all of them as they marched toward him.

"Get back!" Willie waved, still hunched forward from the pain. "All of you!"

But they kept their steady walk toward him, a look

of determination on their faces, and Willie continued his retreat. He eventually found enough energy to stumble away, but he knew he wouldn't be able to make it very far.

Unsure of where to run, Willie headed for the woods, disappearing from the compound before anyone else could sound an alarm. He didn't think they would chase after him. They would simply be glad he was gone.

But as Willie collected his thoughts, his embarrassment and shame compounded his anger, and he knew what had to be done. He reached into his pocket and removed the pistol he'd kept on him since the EMP had been detonated. He didn't like using a pistol. He always preferred his hands to do the talking, but he was willing to make an execption.

Willie looked back to the camp with hot tears in his eyes. If that bitch Carolina thought she was going to have a life without him, she was dead wrong.

14

With the new information given to Ben and Jackson from the nuclear physicist, they didn't waste any time trying to move slowly or quietly on their way toward Johnson City. The only thing that mattered now was recovering that device before it fell into the hands of the leaders of The New Order.

Ben hoped they would catch up with the people who had taken the item, but the farther they rode without running into anyone, the more worried Ben became that it was too late to catch up.

Still, Jackson didn't relent his pace, the man looking more comfortable in the saddle as they galloped down the highway. But when Ben noticed the white foam at the corner of Jackson's horse's mouth, he knew they needed to slow down and take a break.

Ben rode up next to Jackson, catching his attention. "We need to find water! For the horses!"

"Can't it wait?" Jackson asked.

"Not unless you want to walk the rest of the way," Ben answered.

Jackson nodded, but he grimaced in frustration. He slowed the animal, and then he and Ben pulled over. The horses huffed with exhaustion, and Ben led them down to a creek off the road. The ride down was steep, but the animals were surefooted, and they descended without incident.

Jackson and Ben dismounted while the animals drank, but Jackson couldn't sit still. "They could already be in Johnson City by now."

"We don't know that," Ben said, even though he had a similar thought only moments before. "We'll catch up to them."

Jackson grunted and then walked down to the creek bed a few steps away from the horses. Ben understood the colonel's fears. The fact that the enemy they were fighting had managed to set off an EMP was incredible on its own.

But to have the same people who did all of this also have the ability to obtain a nuke was the most dangerous and frightening thing he could imagine. He had seen these people up close, he had fought them, and he knew that their zealot ways would not be deterred no matter what stood in their path.

And caught in the middle of it was Ben's own

brother, someone with whom he had a bad relation-ship, but also secretly wished that they would one day be able to overcome their differences and begin anew. But it didn't look possible now. Whatever small pieces of Mark that Ben had hoped were still in him had been dissolved by the hateful rhetoric of the group he had joined, and Ben had to come to terms with the fact that his brother was too far gone to be saved.

Ben lingered by the horses and glanced down the creek where Jackson had walked, but he didn't see the colonel anywhere along the water's edge. There was a bend not too far ahead where Jackson could have walked around, but Ben didn't know why Jackson would have gone that far.

The horses had finished drinking, and the longer Ben stood there alone, the more his imagination got the better of him. He tied off the horses and took his rifle as he quietly walked down the river's edge.

Ben didn't want to shout the colonel's name lest he cause more trouble than was necessary, and when he finally turned the corner and he still didn't see Jackson, he became frantic.

Ben glanced around, finding nothing but water, rocks, and trees. He spun in circles, feeling the panic grow inside of him. Had Jackson been taken? Did he run away? Was Ben about to walk into a trap?

Questions circling his mind, Ben didn't even notice when Jackson emerged from some bushes and waved to catch Ben's attention. By the time Ben noticed Jackson, he nearly yelled out before he saw Jackson press his finger to his lips to signal quiet.

Ben crossed the shallow creek and joined Jackson on the other side. Jackson gestured up the hill, and Ben followed, being mindful not to make too much noise.

They climbed the hillside opposite the road for a long time, but when Jackson finally stopped at a small plateau, Ben lay on his stomach beside him and saw why Jackson had chosen to be so quiet.

Ahead was a small clearing through a cluster of trees. The narrow opening they were looking through was almost too small to see anything, but once Jackson gently and carefully pulled back some of the bushes, he revealed a large camp.

From what Ben could see, there were a total of six men, all of them armed and all of them wearing the same insignia Ben had seen his brother wear. It was a team from The New Order, but there was no way to tell if this was the same group that had left the prison with the scientist's piece of the nuclear device.

Once Ben had seen what Jackson had found, the colonel motioned for them to back up, and then they quickly but quietly descended the mountain. They hurried back to their horses, and once they were out of earshot, Jackson finally spoke up.

"I think that's them," Jackson said.

"Are you sure?" Ben asked. "Because that could be any one of the dozens of small units The New Order has roaming through the state."

"They're heading in the same direction we are," Jackson said. "Small team, it makes sense. Plus, they are taking a break off the main road. Guys like them wouldn't need to be worried about any locals trying to rough them up; they know how to fight. But they're not taking any chances."

Ben agreed that the camp was made way out of the line of sight from the road. With something as important as a piece to the nuclear device they needed to make the bomb, it would make sense for the unit to take extreme caution on their journey back to the city.

"So we found them," Ben said. "Now, what do we do?"

"We stash the horses, take them out, and grab the nuclear device," Jackson answered.

Ben waited for the rest of the plan, but when none came, it was up to him to point out the obvious. "There are six of them, Jackson. Two of us. Even with the element of surprise, we might not be able to get all of them. Plus, they have automatic weapons. It's a lot easier to shoot a man when you're firing a dozen rounds a second."

"They don't have any guards," Jackson said. "I think this is a quick break before they start the trip again. We might not get another chance at this while they have their guard down."

Ben weighed all the information and knew that if these were the men who had created the device that it would be the golden opportunity to take advantage of, but if they weren't the men, then they would be putting themselves in danger for no reason.

"Look, I would have you sit this one out, but I need you," Jackson said. "I can't take all of those guys on my own. I need your help."

The fact that Jackson was admitting to needing help was almost reason enough to jump in, but Ben still had his doubts.

Ben fidgeted. He didn't know why he was so nervous about this. He understood the risks in coming with Jackson, and he knew how imperative it was for them to find the device, but still, he couldn't shake this feeling.

"It's now or never, Ben," Jackson said. "We need to make a move."

Ben nodded and grabbed the reins of the horses. "We'll stash them farther down toward the bend in the creek in case we need to make a quick getaway."

Once the animals were stashed, Ben and Jackson made sure that all the guns were loaded and ready to go.

"We'll come at them from both sides," Jackson said. "Surround them, make it feel like there are more of us than there really are."

"And what about the device?" Ben asked. "What if someone makes a run for it?"

"We chase them down," Jackson answered. "They're all on foot. But if we make them feel like they're surrounded, then we should be able to keep them pinned down."

Ben nodded. It was risky, but they didn't have a lot of options at this point. "So, once they're neutralized, then we search them?"

"That's the plan," Jackson answered. "I shoot first, so that's the signal. Ready?"

They ascended the mountainside and approached the group of gunmen quietly. They were still in the same positions, still unsuspecting of the imminent attack.

Ben noted the six men all had their firearms nearby, but none of them in the firing position. He began to think that this plan might work, and Jackson and Ben separated to move into their positions.

Ben approached quietly, unsettled at how easily he was now falling into this routine. He had some combat training, yes, but he never imagined he would be using it this much. He had originally gotten into prepping to weather the little storms: economic recession, natural disaster, political unrest, but the idea behind prepping was to act as a stopgap. He never imagined having to live in a world so unsettled as this, and he never wanted to have killed so many people as he had done and was about to do now.

Ben waited in the brush, finger on the trigger as he brought one of the gunmen into his crosshairs. He was anxious, waiting for Jackson to pull the trigger, and he suddenly wished that he had been the one to start the fight.

Waiting to pull the trigger to kill a man was one of the most anxious experiences of Ben's life. But he wasn't sure if it was the actual act of killing the man or the fact that he was doing it so covertly. It made him wonder how many crosshairs he would find himself in the coming days.

The men continued to talk and chat, and one of them burst out laughing, and then all hell broke loose as Jackson fired from the other side of the camp.

Ben didn't pause to see the reactions from the other men, and instead, he just pulled the trigger, putting a bullet through the side of the head of the man who'd been sitting down, engaged in conversation with the rest of his comrades.

Jackson managed to bring down one more before the rest of the group found cover, but Ben missed his next target as he ducked behind a tree.

"Where the hell are they coming from?" One of the men shouted.

"They're fucking everywhere! Just shoot!"

When the men started spraying the forest with bullets from their automatic weapons, Ben flattened himself to the dirt, waiting for a lull in the gunfire. He felt his heartbeat against the soft soil of the earth, and each quick breath brought with the scent of dirt, leaves, and grass. And despite the violence and chaos surrounding him, he had a flash of his childhood appear to him. It surprised him, but he was suddenly in the woods, playing hide and seek with Mark. It was before their parents had died, before everything had turned to shit.

The gunfire ended, and Ben propped himself back up on his elbows. He peered into the scope of his rifle and found the man he'd followed earlier. Only elbows and a piece of the man's shoulder were visible from behind the tree, not enough for a clean shot. Ben remained patient, using the same tactics he used in hunting. Let the prey lull themselves into a trap of their own making.

Ben then saw the fighter look back at the campsite. He was searching for something, and Ben realized that the enemy had left the nuclear device with the rest of the gear.

The enemy exchanged hand signals between them. Ben couldn't see what was signed, but he figured one of them would be making a move toward the package.

Another minute passed, with sporadic gunfire exchange between Jackson and the gunmen who were trapped on his side of the battle. And then a heavy wall of fire erupted as the man Ben was watching sprinted from the cover of his tree toward the camp.

Ben was a pretty good shot, and he easily tracked the runner and kept him in his line site. Once Ben had a good bead on him, he pulled the trigger and shot the man in the stomach. The man collapsed and rolled forward a few cycles before laying completely still.

Ben looked to the bag where the man had been heading toward and figured that's where the piece of the nuclear device was located. Ben needed to get to it before someone else beat him to it.

With three of the other gunmen now dead, the odds were shifting into Ben and Jackson's favor. But with the device so close, it was growing harder to wait for an opening.

Ben couldn't stop shaking. And it wasn't from adrenaline or fear but from hesitation. He didn't think his body could take killing another person. He had lost track of the number of men he had killed, and he was becoming numb to the act of it. He was haunted by the faces of the dead, and he wasn't sure how much longer he would be able to hold it together.

Unable to wait any longer, Ben glanced over to the other shooters and saw that most of their attention was focused on Jackson in the woods. Now was his opening.

Ben quickly got up from the dirt and headed toward the duffle bag next to the man on the ground. He sprinted as fast as he could, but he still felt slow. By the time he reached the halfway mark, the other shooters had noticed, and Ben was suddenly under fire. But he was too close to turn back now, and he reached for the duffle bag, snagging it on the run as he never broke his stride and headed back toward the woods.

Ben's heart skipped from the amount of gunfire that chased him, but he never stopped as he made his way down the hill. He headed for the horses, suddenly in-flight mode and wanting to get out of this place as fast as he could move.

Ben was moving too quickly down the side of the hill, and he lost his footing. He tripped and tumbled head over feet into the water, which helped soften the blow, but not by much.

Ben landed on a few rocks stuck in the soft sediment of the riverbed, one of them cutting his arm. But his body was still so loaded up from the adrenaline that he popped back up as if nothing had happened and looked back up the mountainside to see if the enemy had chased him.

Water dripped from Ben's body as he aimed his rifle up into the trees. He was frozen in his position, ready to shoot at a moment's notice, but the longer he waited, the more he realized that everything had gone silent.

No shooting. No shouts. Nothing.

Eventually, Ben heard movement on the hillside, but when he swiveled his rifle toward it, he saw Jackson coming down. He lowered his weapon.

"Are you all right?" Ben asked.

Jackson said nothing, but he wasn't moving fast enough to warrant someone following him, and he didn't look like he'd been shot. When he reached the creek, he waded out into the water and then punched Ben with a stiff right hook.

Ben stumbled to the left, but he didn't go down. He

rubbed his jaw where Jackson had struck him and then frowned.

"What the hell was that?" Jackson asked. "The plan was to wait until they were all neutralized before we made a grab. You could have blown the whole damned thing!"

Ben knew Jackson's anger was warranted, but he shook his head. "I couldn't—"

"I don't give a damn," Jackson said, marching toward him. "You're lucky I stayed at my post, or the two men who chased after you would have put a bullet in your back on your way down the mountainside."

Ben nodded. "Thanks."

Jackson calmed a little bit. "Did you get it?"

Ben glanced at the duffle bag still in his hand. He walked to the bank and set it down in the mud. He unzipped it and then lifted a bulky metal piece from inside. It was about the length of a baseball bat but looked like an elongated desktop computer, minus the blinking lights.

"That has to be it," Jackson said.

"I can't believe he made this," Ben said.

"Yeah, well, I can't believe that actually worked." Jackson reached for the device and examined it for himself.

Ben looked up the hillside. "They're all dead."

"No," Jackson said, and then he put the device back into the duffle bag. "One of the bastards got away."

"What?" Ben asked, raising his rifle.

"Relax," Jackson answered. "He tailed it in the opposite direction. Didn't even bother looking back. By the time he finds someone to tell, we'll be back in Asheville." He picked up the duffle bag and slung the strap over his shoulder. "Our job is done. Let's go."

As Jackson walked back over to the horses, Ben stared back up the mountainside. He wanted to believe that returning to Asheville would bring a sense of normalcy with it, but he knew that wouldn't be the case. He remembered how relentlessly his brother had tracked him from the prison camp outside of Charlotte. He had no reason to suspect that this time would be any different, especially since they had stolen such an integral part of their master plan.

Nancy was invited to Mrs. Riker's portable with Sarah, Cole, and Mrs. Riker's sister, Rachel. She realized that this was a big moment for her. She had now been brought into the circle. It was validation for all of the hard work she had put in since she had arrived here. They trusted her now, and it felt good to be counted on.

Mrs. Riker paced the floor while everyone else remained seated. Nancy had never seen her this distressed before, and it worried her. She didn't think Mrs. Riker could be this rattled, but the debacle with the food had clearly unsettled her, and rightly so.

"People want to know they're safe," Sarah said. "And we give that to them. I don't understand why you're so worried."

"Because Jane Percy now wants people to think *she*

can keep them safe," Nancy said. "And we need to stop that before it gains momentum."

Sarah rolled her eyes. "You really think Jane Percy stole the food to plant in our portable and blame it on us? Don't you think that's a little… high school?"

"It's an effective way to sow dissent," Mrs. Riker answered. "If it was her, and the more I think about it, the more I agree with Nancy, then she is trying to destabilize the faith in the facility."

"But holding elections?" Rachel asked. "Isn't that a bit… extreme?"

"Yeah, I mean, this isn't going to be a permanent thing, right?" Cole asked.

Nancy studied Mrs. Riker, who was listening to everyone's comments but was also deep in her own thoughts. She couldn't imagine what was going through her mind.

"Mom, are you really worried that you'll lose?" Sarah asked.

Mrs. Riker stopped pacing, and while she had her back turned to everyone else, Nancy saw the look of worry flash across her face before she erased it with a smile and faced the room. "Of course not. I just don't like the idea of restlessness within the community." She rubbed her eyes, trying to make sense of the situation.

"You need to set the tone at the meeting before the vote," Nancy said.

"And how would I do that?" Mrs. Riker asked.

"The Percys are trying to reimagine themselves,"

Nancy answered. "They want to lift themselves up by tearing you down. It's what girls at school used to do all the time whenever they wanted to make someone's life miserable."

"I can attest to that," Sarah said.

"So, you want me to start tearing them down?" Mrs. Riker asked.

Nancy shook her head. "You start tearing them down, and it's only going to make you look like a bully. A lot of the people here don't know who the Percys really are."

"So what does she do?" Cole asked.

Nancy was growing more comfortable now that she had stepped into the spotlight. "You need to be a reassuring pillar of steadiness. You need to be normal. You need everything about your persona to reflect the life that people had before the EMP."

"How do I make myself... more normal?" Mrs. Riker asked.

"Your family," Nancy answered. "You have your family up there with you, and you harp on it as much as you can." She walked over to her and locked eyes with Mrs. Riker. "Because the Percy's aren't a normal family. You start highlighting your own family, and people will start comparing you to them."

"And what makes you think everyone else won't think the Percy family is normal?" Sarah asked.

"Because they're not," Nancy answered. "No matter what kind of show they try to put on themselves, they are not the Cleavers, and they never will be, no matter what they say. I know for a fact that Gray is at odds with his mother. The moment she starts talking about her own family, he will say something, and then we sit back and watch the Percys implode on themselves. People don't want instability in their leadership. They want someone rock solid. That's what you are, Mrs. Riker. And that is what Jane Percy is not."

Nancy smiled, proud of what she had brought to the table, and when Mrs. Riker placed her hand on Nancy's shoulder, she thought she was about to be praised. But she had interpreted her efforts wrong.

"I appreciate the idea," Mrs. Riker said. "But I'm not going to bring the kids into this."

Nancy shook her head. "Your children are already involved. Everybody is involved, and if you don't win this vote, then you risk losing everything. Do you really think Jane Percy will be better for this place?"

"Of course not," Mrs. Riker said. "But I—"

"Then don't lose!" Nancy shouted, losing control of her temper. "You can't just sit there and expect them to play by the rules because they won't! They never play by the rules! They will do whatever it takes to get what they want. I know that firsthand."

Breathless by the time Nancy was finished, she immediatcly realized that she had crossed the line by raising her voice, and whatever clout she had earned looked like it has vanished.

"I appreciate the suggestion," Mrs. Riker said. "But that's not how I'm going to do things."

Nancy stepped back and shrugged. "Fine. If that's how you want to play it, then so be it, but don't blame me when the Percys have control of the facility and you've lost the rest of your family."

Nancy immediately left the portable, storming out of there like she had so many times when she argued with her own parents. She felt like a teenager again, and she hated it. She even hated the tears that were starting to fill her eyes, and she quickly wiped them away.

"Fucking stupid," Nancy said, muttering to herself as she put more distance between herself and the Riker's portable.

Nancy walked all the way to the back fence of the compound, away from the living quarters where there was nothing but some exercise equipment where the firefighter trainees would run their drills on the obstacle course.

Nancy paced around, knowing she had overreacted. She had allowed her own hate toward the Percys to cloud her judgment. Once she had a moment to calm down, and Nancy was able to pull herself out of the pit of despair she found herself wallowing in, she knew she needed to go back to Mrs. Riker and apologize. But when she turned around to do just that, Mrs. Riker was already standing in front of her.

"Oh," Nancy said, shocked.

"How are you doing?" Mrs. Riker asked.

Nancy stared down at her feet, embarrassed from her earlier outburst. "I'm sorry."

"I'm sure you are," Mrs. Riker said, and then she stepped closer. "But that's not what I asked." She grabbed hold of Nancy's hands. "I want to know how you're feeling."

Despite all of the progress Nancy had made since she came here, the moment Mrs. Riker grabbed hold of her hands, she felt like a young girl again. She felt helpless and afraid and angry.

"I keep reliving it," Nancy said. "Watching my parents die."

"I can't pretend to understand how difficult it is to have the Percys stay here after what they did to your family," Mrs. Riker said.

Nancy wiped at her eyes, trying to retain her composure. "I try to keep myself busy so I don't think about it."

"Your suggestion wasn't a bad one," Mrs. Riker said. "I just know how Jane will react once we go down this road. She's not the kind of person to give up, and if I continue to engage with her on her level, then things are going to get worse, not better."

Nancy conceded that Mrs. Riker probably had more experience in dealing with Jane Percy than she did. But she still felt like she had to do something. "I'm just tired of sitting on the sidelines. And I know my little outburst back there didn't set me up for invitations to future meetings, but I want you to know that I'm on your side. Whatever it takes for you to keep control of this place is the necessary action you need to take."

Mrs. Riker studied Nancy for a long time before she finally spoke. "You really have been forced to grow up. You sound like a woman twice your age." She sighed and then pocketed her hands as she turned around to face the rest of the facility. "A part of me wants to do what you suggested, but I have spent my entire life trying to show my own family how to live, and if I stoop to Jane's level, then what am I showing them?"

"That you're a fighter," Nancy answered. "That you will do whatever it takes to keep them safe."

Mrs. Riker turned to Nancy. "I already am like that, Nancy." She placed her arm around Nancy's shoulders and then pulled her close. "Thanks for the reminder, though."

Standing there with Mrs. Riker made Nancy realize just how lucky she was. She could have found herself stuck with some very bad people after all this happened. But she was fortunate enough to have come under the tutelage of decent people.

Nancy was about to express those feelings toward Mrs. Riker when a scream rocketed from somewhere on the compound. Both Nancy and Mrs. Riker immediately sprinted toward the sound of distress.

They followed the noises toward the tents where

the women from the clinic were staying, and it was here Nancy saw Willie with a gun to Carolina's head.

"I want everyone back!" Willie shouted. "Anybody gets close to me, and I will blow her brains out."

The women from the clinic all stepped away, giving Willie the space he requested. Nancy had her weapon drawn, but Mrs. Riker approached with both her hands up in a passive gesture.

"Take it easy," Mrs. Riker said. "Why don't you put down the gun, and we can talk about what it is that's bothering you."

Willie kept hold of Carolina tightly and made sure to press the end of the pistol against her head harder. The pressure causing Carolina to wince in pain.

"You want to know what I want?" Willie asked. "I want the damned respect I should have been given the moment I walked into this place!"

Nancy struggled to lineup her shot. Willie was doing a good job of keeping Carolina in front of him as a body shield. She had hit smaller targets like this before, but never with the stakes so high. One wrong move and the bullet could hit Carolina and kill her.

"You know how much work I've done for this woman?" Willie asked, keeping the pistol jammed against Carolina's temple. "You know how much I've given her? And all I ask in return is the respect that I deserve. Respect she has forgotten all about now that she's come to this fucking place and gotten her head filled with a bunch of ideas that she never would have gotten otherwise!"

Mrs. Riker maintained her distance but slowly and progressively inched forward. "I can understand all of that frustration. Really. But this isn't the way to air all of those grievances, Willie. So why don't you put down the gun—"

Willie raised the pistol and fired a round into the air and everyone jumped, a few of the women screaming. He placed the pistol back against Carolina's head, who was trembling out of control at this point. "I will do whatever the hell I want, however I want to do it. No one here, no woman, is going to ever give instructions to me ever again."

Nancy saw the madness on Willie's face. That mask he was able to wear so well for most of his life was discarded and this was the real person underneath. This was the monster Carolina had been so frightened about.

Whatever thread of civility Willie had been holding onto was now severed, and he had completely lost control. He was going to kill Carolina if they didn't step in, but Nancy couldn't bring herself to pull the trigger lest she might hit and kill Carolina herself.

Nancy took her eyes off the target and looked up at the tower, where she saw the end of the sniper rifle sticking over the side. Whoever was up there might have a better shot, but Nancy didn't know if they were skilled enough to take it.

Mrs. Riker never stopped inching forward, always keeping her attention on Willie. "I'm sorry you've had to deal with all of that." She was placating and submissive, and Nancy knew it was all just for show. "Sometimes women become emotional. You know that, right?"

"Yeah," Willie responded with a scoff. "Too fucking emotional."

"That's right," Mrs. Riker. "My husband hates it when I talk back, and I know I shouldn't, but sometimes when it's that time of the month, I just can't help myself."

"Yeah, you turn into some real bitches when you're on the rag," Willie said.

"We do," Mrs. Riker said. "But a man like you knows how to put us in line, don't you?"

Willie nodded, becoming slightly less agitated. "That's right. I do." He leaned his face away to show the marks on his neck where Carolina had scratched him. "That's what she did to me."

Carolina whimpered. Nancy couldn't believe how fragile she looked. She was like a twig caught in the paws of a bear. All it would take would be one quick movement, and she would snap in half.

"That's terrible," Mrs. Riker said, continuing to lay on the sympathy as she inched closer. There was probably only six feet separating the two of them now, and the closer Mrs. Riker moved toward the danger, the more high stakes the standoff became.

"You deserve a woman who knows how to treat you like the man you're supposed to be."

"That's right," Willie said, buying into the bullshit Mrs. Riker was feeding him. "Someone who appreciates what I do for them, not like her."

"No, not like her," Mrs. Riker said. "Would you consider letting me be that for you?"

Nancy watched as Willie was now completely consumed by Mrs. Riker. He was buying into everything she was saying, but he continued to keep Carolina close, and the gun was still pressed against her temple.

Mrs. Riker extended her hand, maybe only a few feet from the two of them now. "Why don't you take me instead. My husband hasn't been around, and I've been desperate for attention. Do you think you could give me some attention?"

Willie was practically drooling, licking his chops. He nodded, fixated on Mrs. Riker. "Yes."

Mrs. Riker smiled, holding up the rouse very well. "Why don't you let her go. And then you and I can spend some quality time together. Doesn't that sound nice?"

Mrs. Riker was within a foot of them now, and Nancy really thought she was going to pull this off. But then Nancy saw something change in Willie's eye; she knew the threat of danger was far from over.

"I think there's just something missing," Willie said.

"What's that?" Mrs. Riker asked.

Willie leaned a little closer, and his playful expression of desire transformed into anger. "You think I'm a fucking idiot."

"What?" Mrs. Riker asked. "No, I don't—"

"Liar!" Willie retreated out of reach, keeping Carolina even closer now, making any shot from Nancy's angle impossible. "What kind of fool do you take me for? You don't think I know when a woman is playing me?"

"Willie—"

"Save it!" Willie snarled, Carolina still squirming and crying in his arms. "All of you women think you're so clever. You think that your wits will save you when the chips are down, but you want to know what will save you? *A man.* You need a man around to save you, and when there are none, you'll find yourselves vulnerable." He looked down to Carolina, grimacing. "That's the lesson you need to learn." He looked up to shout at the rest of the women. "That's the lesson you all need to learn!" He raised his voice and glanced out to the women from the clinic by the tents, and then finally, he looked back to Mrs. Riker. "And you need to learn that you can't save everyone."

Nancy knew this was the moment. She needed to find a shot and take it. If she didn't, then Carolina was going to die.

Mrs. Riker sensed it as well, and she dropped the act and drew her sidearm, aiming it at Willie. "Let her go, now!"

"Everyone must understand that there are conse-quences when you cross me," Willie said, raising his voice as Carolina sobbed. "A woman must understand her place, and if there is no other man to show them, then I will take it upon myself to do it."

"Willie, I'm warning you," Mrs. Riker said.

Nancy tried to line up the crosshairs over Willie, but each time she thought she was close, Carolina would pass into her line of sight. She had no shot.

Willie pulled Carolina even closer, brought his lips to her ear, and while Nancy couldn't hear what he said, she could read the words on his lips. "Say goodbye, bitch."

The gunshot rang loudly, and everyone jumped, screamed, or gasped. Mrs. Riker lunged forward, tack-ling both Carolina and Willie to the ground, but Nancy remained frozen in shock, the gun still gripped in her hands, arms extended.

After all of the training, everything she had done, Nancy had frozen. She stared at the blood that stained the grass and knew that part of what happened here was her fault. She should have trusted herself to take the shot. She had hit targets like this so many times. But when it counted, she had hesitated. And she would have to live with that for the rest of her life.

But then Nancy watched as Mrs. Riker got up from the ground, holding Carolina in her arms. And Mrs. Riker wasn't holding up a body or a limp corpse. She was holding a very pale-looking—and alive—Carolina.

When Nancy stared at the blood on the ground again, she saw that it was coming out of the side of Willie's head and that it was he who lay motionless on the ground.

Mrs. Riker pulled Carolina away from the gruesome sight of Willie's body and then set her down on the grass to look her over near Nancy. "Are you all right?"

Carolina was trembling, her eyes wide, her pupils dilated. She looked like she was catatonic or about to vomit. But she remained quiet.

"Nancy!" Mrs. Riker shouted as if she had been calling her name for several minutes.

"Huh?" Nancy asked, finally peeling her eyes off of the blood from Willie's head.

"I need you to get everyone back," Mrs. Riker said. "Now!"

Nancy nodded and then realized the crowd had gathered even closer now that the danger had subsided and curiosity had taken control. "Okay, everyone, move back. Let's go, give her some room." She managed to push the people aside, giving Mrs. Riker and Carolina some much-needed space. But what Nancy couldn't figure out was who had pulled the trigger?

She knew for sure that it wasn't her, and the angle of the bullet wound Nancy saw on the side of police had didn't match up with the angle that Mrs. Riker had on him. That meant someone from the tower must have taken the shot. And when she looked up and saw

Jane Percy walk down the last few steps with the sniper rifle in her arms, Nancy's heart skipped a beat.

"Is she all right?" Jane asked, rushing over to join Mrs. Riker, who was looking over Carolina.

"She's in shock," Mrs. Riker answered.

Jane looked back over her shoulder to the dead man. "Bastard. He never should have been let into this place." She stood and saw the approaching crowd. "This is the kind of thing that wouldn't happen under my watch."

Mrs. Riker looked up at Jane and the surrounding crowd listening to her.

"I hope everyone remembers that at the vote later this evening," Jane said, and then she pointed back to Willie's body. "Because we can't afford to have any more of those mistakes walk through our front gates."

Jane walked away, but Nancy saw as the entire crowd watched her leave. She had captured their attention, she had saved the day, and Nancy looked at Mrs. Riker, who realized the same thing she had mentioned before.

Jane Percy wanted to win no matter the cost.

16

*M*ark's unit of men was making good time on their march toward Asheville. He was confident they would arrive in time to set up a scouting party to get a good feel for the military units that were heading their way.

Mark had stopped for a break so as not to tire out his men before the fight. He could already see the signs of battle fatigue on many of the men and didn't want to push them to the brink. They had been fighting nonstop since the EMP had been detonated, and some of the men were growing vocal about their dissent.

And while Mark had his own doubts, he didn't voice them aloud. He needed to stay the course because any hesitation he showed would eventually leak back to the supreme leader, and Mark knew the price of doubt better than anyone. There wouldn't be a third chance for him.

But the longer Mark sat and dwelled on the events that had happened in the previous town, the harder it was to quiet those voices of doubt. They were practically screaming at him now, and Mark found it difficult to concentrate on anything else. He couldn't stop hearing their cries for mercy.

Lost in thought and grappling with his own doubts, Mark did not realize the commotion happening at the perimeter of their encampment.

"Sir," one of the guards Mark had posted to watch the perimeter was catching his breath as he turned to Mark, "we found someone trying to breach our perimeter. He says he needed to speak with whoever is in command. He says it's urgent."

"You confirmed he is one of ours?" Mark asked.

"Yes, sir," the guard answered. "One of our guys trained with him at the program. He's legit. He says it's important. Urgent."

Mark stood. "Bring him in."

"Yes, sir," the guard said and then vanished to fetch the intruder.

Mark paced, unsure what matters this visitor deemed so urgent. It wasn't long before the guard returned with the man they'd found. He was covered in sweat, his face beet red from the exertion of traveling so far on foot. He had come with great haste, and he was still catching his breath.

"Sir," the man said in between gasps, "I was with a team charged with operation Olympus."

There were only a few people within the organization who were aware of that operation and its codename. And it immediately sparked Mark's interest.

"What happened?" Mark asked.

"We were taking one of the finished pieces out of our work camp toward Johnson City," the man said. "We were about halfway there when we stopped for food and water. We were off the main road and out of sight from anybody who might've been traveling. But we were ambushed by a group of men. I'm not sure how many, but they managed to take the device we were transporting to our command center."

Mark's pulse quickened. "You let them take it?"

The man grew fearful. "We were outnumbered. They were shooting at us from everywhere."

Mark clenched his jaw. "And did you actually see these people?"

The man stuttered. "I didn't—I mean I saw—I only saw the person who grabbed the duffle bag, sir."

Mark could have shot the man on the spot. It was a classic divergent technique, making the enemy believe there were more of you than there actually was. "How long ago was this?"

The man cleared his throat. "It took me less than an hour to get here."

Mark grimaced. That was enough time for whoever had stolen it to take off and head to wherever they wanted to go.

"But I think I know where they were going," the man said.

Mark perked up. "And how would you know this?"

The man swallowed, and he grew hesitant as Mark leaned forward. "I, um, I followed them."

"You followed them and didn't recover the item they took?" Mark asked. "Do you have any idea how valuable that item is to the cause? To our supreme leader?"

The man stuttered again, but this time when he finally spoke up again, he had some confidence. "I do, sir. But I explained the situation. We were outgunned—"

"Where were they going?" Mark asked, wanting to cut through the bullshit.

"Asheville, sir," he answered.

The moment the soldier spoke the name of the city, the only thing Mark could think about was his brother. It seemed impossible that Ben was still involved in all of this, but a piece of him knew the truth.

"How do you know this?" Mark asked.

"I met up with the team from the work camp where the device was made," he answered. "We recovered some of the scientists and engineers who escaped during an attack. We think the same people who stole the device were responsible for the attack on the work camp. We interrogated them, and they told us about the city they were talking about returning to."

"Well, that's convenient," Mark said. "Do you still have the scientist you questioned?"

"We brought him with us, but he didn't survive the journey," the man said. "Sorry, sir."

Mark stepped away, needing time to think about his next move. His brother had created this fiasco for him, and Mark remembered what the supreme leader had told him. He would need to take care of this himself. He had sacrificed too much to lose it all now over some nostalgic feeling of brotherly love. It was time to end it.

"Sir?" one of the fighters asked. "Do you have orders for us?"

Mark spun around and saw all the men at his command. He knew they would be able to overwhelm whatever forces waited for him in Asheville, but if his brother was involved with the military somehow, which was the only way any of this made sense, then it wasn't impossible for them to have a few tricks up their sleeve.

But Mark had a few aces in the hole himself.

"How many prototypes do we have finished?" Mark asked.

The soldier frowned. "What do you mean, sir?"

"The work camp where you were stationed was tasked with developing new aerial weapons," Mark answered. "How many did you finish?"

"I don't have the exact numbers—"

"Then find out." Mark leaned forward, enunciating

every syllable, and his underlying tone caused the soldier to immediately depart.

Once he was gone, Mark's right-hand man in the unit approached him.

"Should we dispatch a unit to retrieve the device?" he asked.

Mark considered his answer before he replied. "No." He turned around to face his assistant. "I will handle the retrieval myself."

"Sir, don't you think you should send—"

"I'm perfectly capable of handling this mission on my own," Mark said. "Is that clear?"

The assistant nodded. "Of course, sir."

"Good," Mark replied. "Get the men and tell them to be ready to leave in five."

"Yes, sir!" The soldier quickly saluted and was dismissed.

Alone again, Mark pondered the best way forward. It was obvious to him that if Ben were involved, then he would need to find his brother to find the piece for the bomb. And if Ben were working with the military, he would be well guarded.

But Mark had an ace up his sleeve, and he thought it was time to unleash it against the city that had been the cause of so much pain to him. Mark clenched his fists, letting his anger burn away thoughts of his brother. "They won't know what hit them."

17

*W*illy's body had already been moved, but Nancy stood next to the spot where he had died. There was still blood on the grass, and it was sticky and wet. Every few minutes, she would catch the scent of the claret. It upset her stomach, and she eventually stepped away.

All Nancy had been able to think about since that altercation was how Jane Percy had reacted after she had put a bullet through Willie's skull. It should have been Nancy or Mrs. Riker who had pulled the trigger. But they had missed their chance. And Jane Percy was somebody who never wasted an opportunity.

Nancy knew that this evening would decide the future of every living soul within the confines of the compound. And she still believed that the Riker family were the people to lead them. She understood that she might've had a prejudice against Jane Percy, but even if the woman hadn't killed her mother, then she still would have been hesitant to see her rise to power.

Jane Percy cared about nothing except herself. And she would always only care about herself. And while Nancy respected the fact that Mrs. Riker wanted to keep this as civilized as possible, Nancy knew that Jane didn't care about things like that. And it was up to Nancy to do whatever was necessary to keep Mrs. Riker on top.

Nancy marched through the compound, noting the quiet anxiety that rustled through the air. Everyone was on edge after the altercation with Willie and the impending vote. Most people were outside, talking amongst themselves, and it took her some time to find who she was looking for.

"Hey," Nancy said, trying to sound as friendly as possible.

Gray Percy turned around and smiled brightly when he realized it was Nancy. "Hey!" He gave her a quick look up and down, and she could tell that he still wanted her, so she took the initiative to appease him.

"I am glad I was able to find you," Nancy said. "Do you have a second to talk?"

Gray nodded enthusiastically. "Sure."

Nancy grabbed him by the hand and led him away from the main mess hall. Once they were by the fence, out of earshot for anyone nearby, she lowered her voice. "Do you know what your mother is about to do?" Nancy asked.

Gray stared at her for a minute, silent. "Um, no?"

"She wants to lead this place," Nancy answered.

"Oh, that," Gray replied. "Yeah, I know."

"That can't happen, Gray," Nancy said.

Gray remained timid. She knew he still cared about her. She could always tell when boys liked her. It was one of the skills from her old life that hadn't vanished.

"I know she's done some terrible things," Gray said. "But there's nothing I can do to stop her. She's always done whatever she's wanted."

"You may not be able to stop her, but you can stand up to her," Nancy said, and then she grabbed hold of Gray's hands again, hoping the contact would bring him closer to her way of thinking. "She's going to make a big speech tonight at the compound meeting. When she's finished, you can stand up to her. If people see that her own son doesn't want her to be in charge, then no one will vote for her."

There was the slightest hesitation in Gray's expression, and Nancy feared that she had crossed the line. Perhaps her charms weren't as effective as she believed they would be.

"Nancy, I know you have a problem with my mother," Gray said. "And believe me when I say that I am so angry at her for what she did, but..." He looked away, and Nancy feared she was losing him. "I don't know if I can do something like that to her."

Nancy released Gray's hands. "She is a murderer, Gray. She has killed people, and she's going to keep killing people if she's in charge of this place. No one will be safe, and you know that."

Gray rubbed his forehead, and Nancy could tell that he was distraught over the whole situation. "Nancy, I just don't know if I can cross that line. That's something I will never be able to take back."

"And I will never get either of my parents back," Nancy said, her tone sharp and biting. She could tell her words hurt him and that she was losing his confidence. She stepped closer and wrapped her arms around him. "If I ever meant anything to you, then you will stand up to your mother tonight. Not just for me, but for yourself."

Before Gray could reply, Nancy stood on her to be toes and kissed him. It was a soft peck on the lips, but when Nancy pulled away, and she saw that Gray's eyes were still closed, she knew that she had him.

"Don't let me down, Gray." Nancy let him go and walked away.

She had played her trump card, and she felt dirty for it. But the future of everyone's lives at this place depended on Mrs. Riker winning the vote tonight, and Nancy had done what she could to ensure the win.

* * *

LIZ PACED BACK and forth nervously in the portable. She was alone. Sarah had taken the boys over to Kurt and Susan's place to watch the baby as well as the other children.

The nerves fluttering around in her stomach refused to calm, and Liz had to sit down to try to steady herself. She kept thinking she was about to throw up, but the feeling passed. All she had to do was tell the truth, be honest with everyone. She had to believe that was enough.

But Liz also considered what Nancy had told her. The girl might have had a vendetta against Jane Percy, but that didn't make her wrong about the tactics to use against her to win.

"Ben," Liz said, speaking to herself, "I wish you were here."

But Liz also knew that Ben was off on a mission that was just as vitally important to their livelihood as what Liz was about to do. Still, she kept wondering how he would have handled all of this and then realized that it didn't matter. She was traveling down rabbit holes and paths that had no consequence on the present moment, and the here and now was where she needed to concentrate all of her energy and focus.

Liz stood and then marched toward the door. There was no use in wasting time. She had been in high-pressure situations before, and she knew she would be able to handle this moment, no matter how big it seemed to be.

When Liz arrived at the mess hall, the place was already packed. From what she could tell, everyone had shown up, even Marty. The only person not in attendance was Sarah, who had been tasked with watching the children. Besides her sister, Rachel, Liz had no family present, and she started to regret having Sarah volunteer to watch the kids. She could use the support, but she reminded herself that she still had friends in the audience.

Melissa and Tony Kippers were in attendance, Kurt and Susan were here, along with Cole and Nancy. There were people who she considered on her side, and she just needed to convince the new women who arrived that she and her family had everyone's best interests at heart.

Jane Percy had already arrived, and she was upfront with her husband and brother-in-law, but Liz noted that Gray wasn't sitting with the family, though he was nearby.

Liz met with Jane at the front, and the two had a brief exchange before the proceedings began.

"I'm glad you showed up," Jane said. "I was beginning to think that I would win this by default."

"We don't have to do this, Jane," Liz said. "Our arrangement has worked well enough to skip the theatrics."

"But things aren't running smoothly," Jane said. "That's why we're having the vote. You said it yourself that people deserve to be heard, or are you backtracking on that?"

Liz realized that this was going to happen no

matter what she tried to do. She extended her hand to Jane, and the women shook on it. "Then let's get this started." She turned to face the crowd, wanting to get the first word in before Jane had a chance to completely control the narrative, as she had already done.

"Thank you, everyone, for coming," Liz said. "Today has been a difficult one, so I appreciate you still showing up to voice your concerns." She gestured to Jane. "Jane Percy and I will be speaking with you tonight on who we believe should have your confidence in leading this place. Each of us will speak our peace, and then you will cast your vote anonymously to show who you would like to lead our group. This will be very informal in regards to rules, no time limit, but I would like to ask for everyone to hold their questions until both Jane and I have had a chance to speak." She turned to Jane. "I'll let you go first, Jane." She took a seat before Jane could reject the offer, and all eyes were on her.

Jane Percy stepped up and cleared her throat. "Thank you, Liz. I appreciate you being open to all of this, and I know the community is thankful for it, too." She offered a curt nod to Liz and then turned all of her attention to the crowd.

"I don't think anyone here believes that we would have made it here without the help of the Riker family. They have been more than willing to share resources, and they possessed the knowledge needed for us to pull through the first few weeks after the EMP detonated. But as we move forward, I think it's important for this community to reflect on the foundation that this country was built on, and that is democracy. Our forefathers fought against the same type of tyranny that's plaguing our country at this very moment. And we need to band together in order to fight it. And the reason I'm coming to you all is that I believe I have what it takes to guide us through this next difficult stage of rebuilding what we've lost.

"My family is no stranger to adversity. Our land was pilfered from us from the wealthy and the corrupt. But we've continued to fight throughout the entire process. That's what I bring to the table."

Jane paused for a moment and pointed to Liz.

"Now, I want to talk a little bit more about the kind of job Liz and her family have done. As I mentioned before, they led us to this facility, which, I think it's safe to say, has been a safe haven for all of us. But they've also put themselves in a position of power in the process."

Jane held out her hand. "They are in charge of the food, the weapons, the shelter, security, every piece of vital resources that we need they have one of their own in charge of it." She shrugged. "Is that right? Should the Riker family have a monopoly on our well-being? I don't believe they should, and I think there are a lot of you who agree with me. The consolidation of power and resources puts all of us at risk. Even the Riker's themselves."

Liz tried not to look out at the crowd while Jane spoke. She didn't want to know how much they were eating up her words, but she couldn't help herself as she glanced behind her.

The crowd looked like they were split, with the majority of Jane's support coming from the battered women who had come with Sarah and Nancy from the clinic. But she wasn't sure how many of her old friends would go against her.

"I will make everybody this promise now," Jane said. "If you are to humble me with the position of leading us into a safer and more secure future, I will make sure I bring every single one of you with me on that journey. This will be a place where everybody's voice is heard. Thank you."

The room clapped after Jane had finished, and she returned to her chair next to Lester. Liz stood, her heart hammering in her chest. She couldn't remember the last time she was this nervous. She stood at the front of the mess hall and glanced out into the crowd. She opened her mouth to speak, but her mouth was so dry that she only coughed.

Liz held up her hand and then reached for bottled water. She drank half of it and then set it down. "Sorry about that. It's been a few years since my high school speech class."

There were a few chuckles, and Liz took that as a good sign.

"Some of you know me very well; others don't," Liz said. "But I'm here to talk to everyone tonight. I know Jane has brought up some very good points about what has transpired, and I thank her for the kind word she said about my family." She looked to Jane, and nodded, and saw the narrowed, laser focus gaze from Jane.

"But how well you know me and my family doesn't matter if you don't trust us," Liz said. "And the truth is we have betrayed that trust in some of you. And I'm sorry. But the burden of leadership has landed heavily on my family's shoulders. And you know what? We would welcome more help from everyone here in the community. Because we can't do this ourselves, and we know it. So let this be a new start for all of us. Let your voice be heard, and you choose who you want to be represented. Because my family, and especially me, would love the help."

Liz then held up her finger and paused for a bit of dramatic effect. "And I will make this promise to everyone here this as well: No one gets a free pass. Not me, or my family, or my friends. All of us should be held accountable for our actions. I will always put my money where my mouth is. I have skin in the game, that much I think everyone can agree on."

Liz paused to gauge the response from the crowd and couldn't tell if she was winning anyone over or if it even mattered and people had already made up their minds.

"The path forward will be difficult," Liz said. "But my family and I have gotten us this far, and we will continue to fight for this place no matter what happens. Thank you."

The same amount of applause followed Liz's speech, and she wondered if she had done enough. Once that was finished, they opened it up for anyone who had a question to ask it on the floor.

For a few seconds, no one came up, and then Liz's stomach churned when she saw Wendy Sutton and Marty Schwartz approach the front. Wendy had lost her husband Jeff the day after the EMP when he followed Ben and a few others to the dam to stop it from being destroyed.

And Marty had lost his wife during the attack at Ted Bartman's ranch. Both of them had a bone to pick, and this was the perfect scene for them to air their grievances.

"My name is Wendy Sutton, and the man standing next to me is Marty Schwartz," she said.

Marty remained rigid like a stone, and he refused to look Liz in the eye. Wendy, on the other hand, didn't have any qualms about that.

"My husband, Jeff, was killed following orders from the Riker family," Wendy said. "No one trusted them more than I did, but Ben Riker left my husband to die."

Liz started to stand. "Wendy, I—"

"You don't get to talk now!" Wendy shouted, pointing at Liz. "You had your time. Now, this is our time!"

Liz held up her hands in apology and returned to her seat, realizing that she shouldn't have said anything, to begin with.

Wendy cleared her throat and regained her composure. She placed her hand on Marty's shoulder. "Marty lost his wife after she was assigned to a very dangerous post, killed by the same enemy that triggered the EMP that started all of this."

Marty bowed his head, and Liz could tell he was barely holding it together. She knew how hard Ali's death had been on him, but the man refused any help she tried to offer. And now he was dead set on focusing all of his grief on wounding Liz and her family, and indirectly, the compound.

"And the same enemy that killed our loved ones has been living right here, in this very building," Wendy said, referring to Abe. "The Rikers have treated that man like a guest!" she scoffed. "He is an animal, and he deserves to be put down. Keeping him alive is an insult to everyone we've lost."

Liz had thought Abe might come up in a discussion, but she had thought Jane would bring it up, but Wendy was doing all of Jane's dirty work for her. All the while, Jane looked like she was taking the high road, just like Nancy tried to get her to do.

"I know what a lot of you are probably thinking,"

Wendy said. "That our loved ones suffered unfortunate fates. The truth is that they should have never been in those situations in the first place. The Riker family has taken unnecessary risks, putting everyone's lives in danger. Now, I have spoken to Jane Percy myself, and I am certain that she would never put anyone of us on the front line without proper protection and training." Wendy straightened up and lifted her chin. "I have known Liz Riker for almost ten years. And I want everyone here to know that I will be casting my vote for Jane Percy." She touched Marty's shoulder again. "And so will Marty. Thank you."

Wendy offered one final piercing gaze at Liz before she marched down the aisle with Marty next to her, and they returned to their seats.

Liz could feel the mood in the room shift, and she knew there was nothing she could say that wouldn't only make things worse. Unless she apologized.

When Liz stood, the murmuring stopped. Every single person was looking at her, and never before had she felt the weight of leadership as she did at that moment.

"Wendy, Marty," Liz said, taking a breath, "I am so sorry for what happened to Jeff and Ali. I cannot fathom your loss." She bowed her head, picking at her fingernails, a nervous habit she developed in high school whenever she had to make a public speech in class. "I know that if I lost Ben, I would be just as furious and angry at me as you are." She looked up and felt the tears gathering in her eyes. She wasn't sure if the people would think it was for show or that they were genuine, and in that moment, she didn't care.

"My husband, Ben, is currently out on the front lines, securing the future for not just his family, but for everybody in this facility. Or my daughter, who puts herself at risk every time she goes out to gather supplies to keep us alive. My family fights for this place, and they fight for you. You never asked us to, but we answered the call anyway. The world is a dangerous place now, and no matter what we do, there will always be a level of danger to this life. But don't let your decisions be guided by fear. I can promise you nothing good ever comes from that."

Liz lingered for a moment and then returned to her seat. She had said her peace, done what she could, but only time would tell if it would be enough.

"I have something to say."

Liz turned along with every other head in the room, and her eyes widened in both surprise and fear when she saw Gray Percy standing up. He looked to his mother on his way to the front, and Liz noticed how tense Jane looked.

Liz looked over to Nancy, who remained focused on Gray as he took his stand at the front of the room. He looked nervous, and he avoided eye contact with his mother. Liz expected Jane to intervene, but then she realized by interfering, Jane would be causing more trouble and going against everything she had just preached about everybody having a voice. She couldn't silence someone in her own family without looking like a hypocrite.

"My name is Gray Percy," he said. "Jane is my mother."

Jane forced a smile, but even from a distance, Liz could tell that she was furious.

"My mother made a big speech about how dangerous the Riker family is," Gray said. "What she failed to mention was the fact that she's a killer herself."

Jane immediately stood up as the room broke out in whispers. Lester grabbed her arm and gently pulled her back down into her seat.

"She, along with my father, Lester Percy," Gray said. "Both of them killed the parents of one of the very members of this community. I am ashamed to admit that happened, and I can only apologize to a friend for the atrocity committed against her family." Gray found Nancy in the audience and looked at her but didn't speak her name. "I'm sorry."

Liz couldn't believe that Nancy had gone behind her back and spoken to Gray anyway. But there would be a time for that conversation later.

"My parents are not the people to lead this community," Gray said. "But I hope that one day they can atone for all the terrible things they've done. And I hope they take the words I'm speaking now to heart. Because that's where they come from." Gray turned toward his mother and father. "I love both of you. And

I hope that one day we can forgive each other." He turned back toward the crowd. "That's all I have to say. Thank you."

Once Gray returned to his seat, the room continued to buzz with whispers. It appeared that both candidates now had their dirty laundry flapping in the wind. The only question left was who the community would choose as the better option.

Small sheets of paper were passed out along with pencils. The names were written on the paper and dropped into a shoebox. Once all the names were collected, the votes were counted by a member of the Riker family and a member of the Percy family.

Jane had chosen her brother-in-law, Danny, and Liz had chosen her sister, Rachel. Once both of them confirmed the numbers, they both walked up to the front of the room, and everyone fell silent.

"We have the final count," Rachel said.

Danny cleared his throat. "We have seventeen votes for Jane Percy."

Liz felt her stomach doing backflips, and she clutched the armrests, wishing that one of them was Ben's hand. She had never felt more alone waiting for those results, but when she looked at Rachel and saw the hint of a smile spread across her face, she felt the tightness in her chest relax.

"And nineteen votes for Liz and Ben Riker," Rachel said.

There was a mild manner amount of applause, and

Liz felt Cole grab her shoulder. She smiled at him and then stood, waving to the rest of the community. She found Jane Percy, who looked like she wanted to murder Liz, but the pair shook hands, and then Liz gestured for everyone to sit down.

"Thank you," Liz said. "Thank you very much. I appreciate your confidence in my family to continue to lead us. And I want you to know that no matter who you voted for, my top priority, and the priority of my husband, is to ensure the safety and survival of everyone in this community. Thank you again."

Liz bowed, and the place erupted in applause once more. But not before Liz caught the death stares from Wendy and Marty on their way out. Even though she had won the vote, Liz had a sinking feeling that people had now drawn their lines in the sand.

18

*T*he entire ride back to Asheville, Ben couldn't stop thinking about what they were carrying. They had managed to find a piece of a nuclear bomb that a domestic terrorist group was going to detonate in some major city. At least that's what Ben believed they wanted to do.

As they returned to the burnt and decimated city of Asheville, Ben was reminded of the level of destruction the enemy was capable of achieving. If they could do all this with nothing but normal weaponry, he couldn't imagine the type of destruction that would occur if they managed to detonate a nuclear bomb. Life as they knew it would be altered forever. Not that it hadn't been altered significantly already.

Ben caught up to Jackson, who had maintained a hellish pace back to the city. The colonel was eager to meet up with the rest of his military comrades and deliver the item and the news of what they had found.

But as they entered the city limits, Asheville looking as desolate as it had before they left, Ben wondered if the military was going to show up at all.

"Where are they?" Ben asked.

Jackson didn't sound worried when he answered, but Ben saw the hesitation on the colonel's face. "I'm sure they are working on setting up a position inside the city."

"You're certain that the orders you received were the correct ones?" Ben asked.

Jackson glared at Ben. "Orders are orders. I don't have the luxury to pick and choose my missions."

Ben shook his head. "Last I recall, I didn't have much choice in the matter of coming with you. And it would be nice if you dropped the holier than thou act. I don't think we need to be comparing who is more willing to sacrifice their life for their country. Because I would sacrifice my life to save my family. They are everything to me. And I only agreed to this because you said the military would be here to back up my family."

The colonel simply kicked his horse and spurred the animal forward, racing into the city. It seemed Jackson wasn't as confident as he had led on.

Ben considered returning to the compound without going into the military camp. It was getting later, and he was hoping to return home before sundown, but he didn't want to go home empty-handed. He knew how much they needed military support, especially if the enemy returned in full force, which Ben knew they would.

Ben wished his brother had never joined The New Order. It had made a bad situation worse, but Mark had always wanted to walk his own path. Ben just never believed that his brother would choose a path so violent and destructive.

Despite his desire to go home, Ben followed Jackson into the city. It had been a while since he had returned to the city since the fires.

Cars were blackened and charred. Signs in front of buildings were melted. Glass was shattered, the contents inside all the stores just as scorched as the rest of the city. It was like walking through a graveyard or some post-apocalyptic movie that should have always remained fiction. Except this was their reality.

A thin film of soot still layered the entire city. Ben thought it might be a stain that would never wash out, no matter how many times it rained. The city had been fundamentally changed, as had the country. It was one of those moments where there was a clear before and after. Even if they managed to return to any semblance of normalcy, the psyche of the nation would be altered forever.

Jackson slowed his pace once they were inside the city limits. Ben thought that maybe he believed the enemy had already come through, but from the intelligence they had been given, the enemy wasn't due through here until tomorrow. The military had the entire day to ready themselves for the impending fight.

"They should have been here by now," Jackson said, finally speaking aloud his worry.

"Maybe they're on the other side of the city," Ben said.

Jackson remained quiet, and they continued to trot through the streets, the clacking hooves from their horses the only noise in the eerily silent city.

Ben saw no human tracks in the soot on the road or anywhere along the sidewalk and knew that no one had walked through here, for at least today. It was odd not seeing any human footprint other than the decaying structures that surrounded them.

"Maybe you should go back to your base," Ben said. "Maybe orders were changed?"

"They wouldn't have changed orders this important," Jackson answered. "This would be the first real strike back against the people who did this. That's not something my commanders would have given up."

Movement up ahead caused both Jackson and Ben to stop their horses. Jackson drew his sidearm, and Ben grabbed his rifle. He had practiced shooting on horseback before and was comfortable dropping the reins to use both hands to hold the rifle.

"Do you see anything?" Jackson asked.

Ben scanned the road through the scope but

couldn't find anything in his crosshairs. "It could have just been an animal."

"Identify yourselves!" a voice yelled from up ahead.

"Colonel Jackson with the second division," Jackson replied. "We are here with classified intelligence."

"Both of you lower your weapons," the voice yelled.

Ben ignored the command. "I can't see anyone. We need to wait and make sure these people are actually in the military."

"I'm afraid we're both a little skittish," Jackson said. "Hard to tell who is friendly and who is foe these days."

The voice went quiet, and Ben still hadn't been able to identify their location. The city walls and building were throwing the guy's voice around, making it difficult for Ben to pin it down.

"We have a bead on you, so when we come out, if you shoot us, our guys will take you down," the voice said.

"Fair enough," Jackson answered.

A few seconds later, Ben watched as two men, dressed in military fatigues, stepped out of what used to be a clothing store that Ben had visited with his boys. They carried the brand of T-shirts that they liked to wear.

"Lower your rifle," Jackson said.

"You're sure these guys aren't just dressed like the military?" Ben asked.

Jackson nodded. "They're the real deal."

Ben slowly lowered his rifle, but even with the

colonel's assurances, he still felt exposed. It wasn't until the pair were directly in front of them and they shook hands with Jackson that Ben finally relaxed.

"What kind of high-priority intelligence have you brought us, Colonel?" the soldier asked.

Jackson lifted the duffel bag off of the horse's sidesaddle and dropped it into the arms of the soldier. "You can thank us later for preventing another Armageddon."

The pair of soldiers exchanged a glance, and then Ben and Jackson followed the soldiers back to their checkpoint and then into the camp.

The military unit had chosen to take refuge in the remnants of an outlet mall. It was big enough to fit all of their people, and with men strategically placed on the roof, they were able to see far ahead on the outskirts of the city. Not to mention the outlet strip mall was still fairly intact and provided shelter from the elements.

Ben and Jackson tied off the animals outside of the mall and followed the soldiers inside. They received some strange stares, and as Ben studied the faces of the soldiers he passed, he knew these guys had it rough.

Face after face stared back at Ben with sullen anger. Ben knew that these military units were not accustomed to being on the losing end of a fight. The fact that one of the greatest military superpowers the world had ever seen had been fooled by a ragtag team that was no more than a militia hadn't set well with anyone.

But Ben suspected that the military wasn't going to make that same mistake again.

Ben followed Jackson into a large tent that had been set up at the center of the outlet mall. When they entered, Ben figured it was the command center because he saw a map set up in the center of the room with a group of officers standing around it, pointing at different structures, no doubt determining where they believed the enemy was going to make their next attack.

"General McGuire," the soldier who led them inside saluted a gray-haired man. "I have Colonel Jackson with the second division reporting, sir."

The general saluted the soldier and then dismissed him. Jackson stepped forward and offered his own salute.

"General," Jackson said in a stern voice.

"At ease, Colonel," McGuire said. "I was told you have something important for me."

"Yes, sir," Jackson replied. "We received intelligence about a potential nuclear device in play. We managed to secure one of the components before the device could be completed." He gestured toward the duffel bag they had brought in. "I'm not exactly sure what that piece of the device does, we had schematics, but I'm not sure if they made it to you or not."

"No, they did not," General McGuire answered.

Ben and Jackson exchanged a glance, realizing that

the scientists were either dead or had decided to go their own way.

McGuire, along with his advisers, opened the duffel bag and inspected the contents, though Ben was certain none of them understood what they were looking at.

"Jesus," McGuire said. "I want a unit ready to transport this to our research division. This is the highest priority, top-secret clearance."

"Yes, sir!" The young soldier hurried out of the tent.

Once the young man was gone, the general turned to Ben, who was the only person in the room not dressed in military fatigues.

"I don't suppose you have top-secret clearance?" McGuire asked.

Ben shook his head. "No, sir, but I can keep a secret."

The general laughed. "I suppose that's good enough in times like these. Now, who the hell are you?"

Jackson explained the situation, and Ben chimed in when it was necessary. After they were finished, the general gave Ben another good look up and down.

"So you have a community here that you believe could be in trouble," McGuire said.

"The enemy knows where my family is located, sir," Ben said. "I know it's only a matter of time before they come back and take another shot at us. I was lucky before, but we don't have the numbers to fend off a full-blown attack from these people."

"If I may, sir," Jackson said. "Despite some of the setbacks I've had in my relationship with Mr. Riker, I can vouch for his honesty. He didn't have to return to me at his own risk, but he did. And I couldn't have recovered the nuclear device without his help. He was instrumental in that regard."

Ben was surprised by Jackson's kind words, but he wasn't sure if it was enough to convince the general to help him.

"Mr. Riker, I am not a man in the kind of position in power where I can start diverting resources, despite what my rank might suggest," McGuire said. "But I can promise you right now that your people are safe. I'll send a unit over to collect your people and keep them here until the fighting is finished. You will be well behind our lines and away from any danger before the fighting starts."

The wave of relief that spread throughout Ben's body was euphoric. It was like knowing that his child was sick and then hearing the doctor tell him that they were going to be okay.

"Thank you, General," Ben said.

"Now, if you'll excuse me, I need to get back to planning on how to wallop these bastards," General McGuire said. "When my aid returns, I'll have him find you outside and begin setting everything up."

"Yes, sir," Ben said.

Jackson lingered behind for a little bit to answer a few more questions for the general, and when Ben stepped out of the tent, he thought that he was going to pass out from joy. Despite the danger that still lurked around every corner, Ben knew that this was a step in the right direction. Now that the military was becoming more actively involved, Ben didn't think that the enemy would be up to last much longer. Especially now that they were aware of the nuclear bomb that had to have been the ace in the hole for The New Order.

Ben couldn't wait to get back to his family. Even though it had only been a day, it felt like much longer since he'd actually seen them. Because while they had been together, he hadn't spent any quality time with his wife or his children. He was going to change that the moment he returned.

When Jackson stepped out of the tent, Ben waved and caught the colonel's attention. "You made quite the impression with General McGuire."

"I'm just glad we were able to get done what we needed to." Ben shook Jackson's hand. "Pleasure doing business with you."

Jackson laughed. "I wish I could say the same. Do you have someone walking you out?"

"I'll just hang out here," Ben said.

"Suit yourself," Jackson said. "I'm hitting the mess hall. Though, I have to say you're not missing much. Good luck to you, Ben."

"You too, Jackson," Ben answered.

Ben watched Jackson disappear, and he didn't envy the colonel's continued role in the coming fight. But it wouldn't be much longer before the fight was over for Ben.

After everything that had happened since the EMP was detonated, Ben was looking forward to taking it easy for a while. He knew it was still going to be difficult. He didn't expect a walk in the park after all of this was over, but he didn't believe that they would face the same level of danger moving forward. It was nice to know that they were no longer alone in this fight.

Ben was so distracted by his own relief that he didn't notice the commotion happening around him until Jackson grabbed hold of his arm, pulling him in a random direction.

"What the hell is going on?" Ben asked.

"The enemy is here, now," Jackson answered.

Ben watched as units mobilized around him. The camp suddenly broke out into a frenzy. "I need to get back to my family."

"Negative," Jackson said, reverting to his military jargon. "The frontline is closed. Everybody is heading toward the fight. Find someplace to lay low, and we can pick up your family after this is done."

Ben yanked his arm free and put space between himself and Jackson. "I did all this to save my family from the danger that's heading right toward us."

"Our scouts tell us that the enemy is heading straight for the city," Jackson said. "There's no reason to believe that your family will be in any danger across the river."

That was the only assurance that Ben received, and as he watched the mass of soldiers around him mobilize and head toward the front line, there was a noise above them. Ben glanced up to the sky, shielding his eyes from the lowering sun, and saw dozens of objects above them.

Ben suddenly remembered the drawing he saw of the crude-looking airplane just as the first bomb dropped.

he moment after the vote ended in the mess hall, Jane Percy wanted to rush over to Liz Riker and snap her neck. But she forced a smile and shook hands. She couldn't believe she had lost. She was convinced after Wendy and Marty had spoken, no one would cast their vote for Liz. The moment she was out of the public eye, she dropped the mask and was seething anger. "What the hell was he thinking?"

"The Rikers must have talked to Gray," Lester said. "Got in his head."

Liz stopped and shook her head. "I know Liz Riker better than that. She wouldn't involve the children. She would think that she's above all that." She snarled. "It was that girl."

"What girl?" Lester asked.

"Nancy Simmons," Jane answered, looking at her husband. "The girl whose parents were killed. She must have spoken to Gray, convinced him to say something tonight. He's still head over heels for that girl even though she's moved on. Clever little bitch."

Jane saw Gray coming out of the mess hall. He was alone, and Jane took the opportunity to rush over and pull him aside. He didn't try to resist, not that Jane gave him much of a choice. Once they were out of sight from everyone else, she tore into him.

"How could you do that?" Jane asked. "To your own flesh and blood?"

Gray wore a mixture of shame and anger. It was obvious he had been conflicted but not conflicted enough to convince himself not to go through with it.

"Look at me, boy!" Jane shouted.

Gray finally looked up. He could barely meet his mother's gaze, but he was strong enough to hold it once he did. "I told the truth."

"The truth?" Jane asked. "Seems to me that you left out a whole piece of truth."

"You killed Nancy's parents," Gray asked.

"Because they threatened us!" Jane answered, raising her voice, and then quieted herself. "It was convenient of you to leave out the fact that Nancy's mother was about to kill you and her own daughter!"

"That doesn't excuse what you did," Gray said.

"But you're excused for cherry-picking the truth?" Jane asked, shaking her head. "No, son, it doesn't work that way."

Jane was a mix of emotions standing in front of

Gray, but of all the pain and anger swirling through her, what she felt most was betrayal.

"I would lay down my life for you, Gray," Jane said. "Without question, in a heartbeat. I would go to the ends of the earth to protect you because you are a part of me." She tapped against her breastbone. "But what you did tonight... I will never forget, no matter how much I want to."

Jane saw the disappointment on her son's face and knew that she had wounded him. But as she walked away, she knew she needed time to process what he had done. Because the anger was coursing through her veins frightened her. She wasn't sure what she would do and chose to remove herself from the situation before she did something she couldn't take back.

By the time Jane returned to her portable and shut the door, not much had changed in regard to her mindset. She was still upset about what Gray had done. It was rare for her to ever feel like she was lost and floundering, but as she sat down on the edge of her cot, that's exactly how she felt.

Lester entered, Danny staying outside for a moment. He remained by the door for a long time. He was never good with words or saying the right thing at the right moment. But the simple fact that he was here made Jane feel slightly better.

"I guess my plan didn't work," Jane said.

Lester walked over and joined Jane on the edge of

the bed. "Nobody could've seen that coming. Not even you."

Jane shook her head. "I knew he was upset. But for him to say something like that, to do something like that, he was much further gone than what I thought."

Lester put his arm around Jane, and she leaned into his side. She had never been one for being coddled, but this was one instance where she didn't mind.

"That was our one chance in trying to do this the peaceful way," Jane said. "After that display from Gray, the damage is done."

"The vote was very close," Lester said. "You don't think that another vote would put you over the finish line?"

Jane leaned away from Lester and looked up at him. She knew he was hesitant about getting into any business with his father. And she didn't like it any more than he did, but they had to play the cards they were dealt. "It's the only way."

Lester stood and paced anxiously. "I know you think that we don't have any other options, but we should make sure we exhaust everything before we go back to him. Because once he knows our plan didn't work, he's going to leverage our failure against us."

Jane had never been one to hold back or offer a sympathetic word, but she knew better than to pit the man she loved against his own father. That was a relationship as complicated as the one she had with her own family.

"I know what your father is, Lester," Jane said. "I know we can never trust him."

Lester turned to face her, and she saw the fear on his face. He was terrified of who and what his father was, and despite the years that had passed, he reverted back to the frightened boy who was abused at the hands of his dad.

"You don't know what he can do," Lester said. "Not really."

Jane walked over to him and gently held his face. "Using him will make things easier for us. Trust me."

Lester placed his hands over Jane's and took a breath. "You've always known what to do. You've always been able to lead us forward. And if you think this path is the way to go, then I'm all in."

Jane kissed him. No matter what he said, this was the foundation of their relationship. They believed in one another. They were a team to the very end. And nothing was going to break that up, ever.

Jane walked outside and told Danny that they needed to speak with Buford. Danny led them back out into the woods and toward the meeting point where they had all gathered before.

Jane and Lester hung back while Danny retrieved his father. Jane made sure to only have Buford return with him because she didn't want to deal with the rest of his posse. It was important for them to set the ground rules with him beforehand. Because she knew

Buford would most likely try to wrangle his way out of the negotiations.

When Danny returned with Buford, Jane saw the smugness on his face. It was exactly how Lester had described. The fact that they had come back meant their plan had failed. But Jane had no intention of letting Buford use it as leverage.

"So, I take it things didn't go well," Buford said.

"Let's just say we're looking at all of our options," Jane replied. "Are your guys still with you, or have they left for greener pastures?"

Buford laughed. "Never willing to admit a mistake. I respect that."

"I'm beginning to think that this meeting was a mistake," Jane said.

"Don't be like that, Jane," Buford said.

"Here's the deal, Buford," Jane said. "We need to stack the odds in our favor at the facility. We've managed to get things moving, but we need one final push over the finish line."

"And you want to use my people to help you do that," Buford said, crossing his arms. "What kind of job are we looking at?"

"We have a prisoner inside the compound," Jane said. "He's a former member of the organization who detonated the EMP. He's being used to gather intelligence against his people, but not everybody is comfortable with him being around. I want to use that to our advantage."

Buford narrowed his eyes. "What did you have in mind?"

"I want you to hurt one of the people in the camp," Jane answered. "And then we're going to blame the prisoner for the mugging."

"Won't people be able to figure out it wasn't the prisoner?" Buford asked.

"It doesn't matter if they find out," Jane answered. "By the time tempers calm down, the damage will already be done."

Buford smiled. "Classic hornet's nest. You stir everything up, and by the time people know what's what, you already have what you came for. Smart."

Jane walked to Buford and stared up at the big man. It looked like a scene from David versus Goliath in regards to their size comparison. But Jane had never been someone to back down or be intimidated simply because she didn't have the size in the fight. And she wanted to make sure that Buford understood who was in charge.

"I want to make it clear that your people understand that this is a surgical operation," Jane said. "One person goes in, they do their job, and then they leave."

Buford stood his ground. "And how will your people know it was this prisoner who roughed up your guy?"

"You let me worry about that," Jane answered. "You just need to pick your best guy, and we'll go from there."

"When is this happening?" Buford asked.

"Now," Jane answered.

Buford raised his eyebrows and laughed. "You don't waste any time. I like that. I'll be back with one of my best."

Once Buford was gone, and it was just Jane, Lester, and Danny, Lester looked more worried than before.

"Do you really think this is the best idea?" Lester asked. "How are we supposed to frame a man who's locked away?"

"Liz's brother-in-law is still in charge of watching the prisoner until this evening," Jane said. "I know for a fact that Cole is seeing Jane's sister. All we have to do is get her to call him, and he comes running. That's our opening. We don't actually have to let the prisoner out. Just have to make it look like no one was there to watch him. Then, we pretend we caught him and take him back before anyone notices. With no witnesses, it will be his word against everyone else's. And there are already a lot of people who don't like him. The odds are stacked against him."

"So what happens after people think Abe roughed someone up?" Lester asked.

"The Rikers will defend Abe, if only for the fact that they need him for more information," Jane answered. "And that's when we go in hard with the counter punch and stoke the flames of dissent. This will be the final straw that breaks the camel's back. One last ineptitude of a family who has failed the community over and over again."

"If it doesn't work?" Lester asked.

Jane clenched her fists by her side. "Well, then we do it your father's way. We have more fighters than they do. So we take the damned place."

20

*A*fter the vote had ended, Marty immediately returned to his portable. Wendy had tried to stop him, talking to him about how none of this was fair and that the Rikers needed to pay for what they had done to their families.

Marty had hoped he would experience some kind of vindication after publicly sticking it to the Riker family, but at that moment, all he felt was empty.

All of the rage and anger he had felt since Ali's death, all of which he had directed at Ben for sending her to that place, had vanished. There was nothing but a pit left behind from where there should have been hope. But none of that mattered now.

A naïve part of Marty believed he would feel better, but that was only the anger talking. He was only going to bury himself deeper into a pit of despair the longer he kept digging at that anger, and soon he wouldn't be able to pull himself out.

But if he lost himself down there, then he knew he would lose his girls. And that was something he couldn't do.

Marty walked over to the Riker's portable, where Sarah was watching all of the children. He was about to knock on the door when he heard laughter inside. He paused, fist in the air. It was Isabelle. He'd recognized that laughter anywhere.

It had been a long time since Marty had heard Isabelle laugh. And Marty knew that he hadn't been the most cheerful person to be around.

It almost felt wrong to interrupt such joy and laughter, but Marty needed his children, and there was still that big part of himself where he felt the anger at the Rikers for what they had done. It was going to take time for that to go away.

Marty knocked, and Sarah answered the door. When she saw it was him, she immediately stopped joking around with the girls and grew serious.

"Hi, Mr. Schwartz," Sarah said.

Marty knew Sarah had nothing to do with what had happened to his wife, but he couldn't stop himself from keeping with the cold shoulder. He simply looked past her and called for his daughters. "Isabelle. Maya. Come."

The girls immediately stopped playing, and the joy they had emitted only moments before was gone.

Never before did Marty ever think that the sight of him would cause his daughters to be disappointed.

"Bye, girls," Sarah said.

Both of the girls hugged Sarah before they stepped outside. Marty could see that they didn't want to go, and it was clear they were having a good time.

Marty looked at Sarah and nodded. "Thank you," Marty said. "For taking care of them."

"Of course," Sarah said.

Marty wanted to say more, but it was getting late, and he didn't have the energy to strike up a conversation. He turned around, took his girls by the hand, and headed back to his portable. The girls said nothing on the walk back. They had grown used to silence. And after hearing them both laugh so hard, so joyfully, Marty hated himself for what he had done to them.

"Girls," Marty said, slowing to a stop. "How would you like to spend the night with Auntie Sarah?"

Both of the girls brightened immediately. They looked up at their father with beaming smiles.

"Really?" Isabel asked.

"Would you like that?" Marty answered.

Both the girls jumped, squealing the same answer of yes. Their joy actually broke through the melancholy that had plagued Marty since Ali's death. They turned around and headed back toward Sarah's portable. When he knocked on the door, and Sarah saw them, she flashed concerned.

"Is everything okay?" Sarah asked.

"I was hoping the girls could stay with you tonight," Marty said. "They were having such a good time, and I hate to take away from that."

Sarah smiled. "Of course. We can have a slumber party."

Both the girls jumped and squealed with delight. "Yay! Slumber party!"

Marty smiled, and his daughters hurried inside the portable. Once they had jumped on the bed and were giggling, Sarah turned around.

"Thank you," Marty said. "I haven't been much fun to be around lately."

"Mr. Schwartz, I can't imagine how hard this has been for you," Sarah said. "Ali was an amazing person with a beautiful soul. And I see her smile in both of the girls."

Marty felt the tears gathering in his eyes. His voice caught in his throat when he answered. "I appreciate that. I'll swing by and collect them in the morning. But if they become too rambunctious this evening, just come and get me."

When Marty returned to his portable, he sat down on the cot and closed his eyes. He needed to find a way out of the darkness that he had crawled into. But he was lost and didn't know which direction he should go.

Ali had always been his compass. No matter what was going on, he could always count on knowing that she would help him down whatever path they walked. But now that he was walking alone, he didn't know what to do. He had wandered from the safe path and landed in dangerous forests. He hadn't even cried since he had found out she was gone. It was like all the anger and hate had blocked any attempt for grieving.

But as he thought about what he had done tonight, how he had betrayed one of his oldest friends, and what Ali would say to him about that, he felt nothing but shame.

"I'm so sorry," Marty said. "I never should have left you."

The first tear broke free in the corner of his left eye and rolled down his cheek. The next tear followed shortly after, and before he knew it, he was bawling silently to himself. He made no attempt to stop his tears because he knew that he needed to feel this. It was an important step into moving on, and that was something he desperately needed to do.

Once Marty had finished crying, he wiped his eyes and reached for one of the small liquor bottles stashed beneath his mattress. He drank the entire thing and then dropped the bottle onto the floor. He closed his eyes, feeling incredibly tired and groggy. It was like someone had given him a drug to relax, and it was currently pumping through his body. All of the tension that he'd been holding inside had finally relaxed.

Marty was about to fall asleep when there was a knock at the door. He forced himself to get up, thinking that maybe the girls needed something. He hadn't thought to give them any other change of clothes or any of the toys that have been found in the city to help give the children some form of entertainment.

Marty opened the door, expecting Sarah, but instead, he was bum-rushed by someone and immediately gagged.

Marty landed hard on his back, and the back of his head cracked against the floor, causing the room to spin. Before he could get his bearings, the man who had tackled him, a man whose face he couldn't see in the darkness, punched him hard in the face.

The sound of broken cartilage and bone proceeded a warm gush of blood that covered Marty's mouth. He stuck his hands up to try to defend himself, but the man continued to beat him with a fury of punches along his ribs.

Marty thrashed, trying to escape, but the man was too big for him to buck off. Every blow to his body sent an explosion of pain through him, and in his disoriented state, he reached to his left and right, trying to grab anything to use as a weapon.

Eventually, his numbing fingers fumbled over something sharp, and he stabbed the man hard in the arm. The attacker cried out and then removed the small cutting blade from his arm. Marty tried to use the moment as a distraction to escape, but before he could make it, the attacker jammed the blade down into Marty's back.

Marty opened his mouth to scream, but the pain

was so intense that he barely gasped. The attacker then flipped Marty over and repeatedly stabbed him in the stomach. The first few stabs were painful, but after that, Marty grew numb until he felt the life draining from him, and he slowly slipped into the cold grip of death to be reunited with his beloved wife.

* * *

JANE PACED HER PORTABLE NERVOUSLY. Lester was with her, but Danny was still waiting by the fence where they had snuck in one of Buford's men.

"He should be finished by now," Jane said.

"I'm sure it's fine," Lester replied.

But Jane shook her head. "Maybe this was a bad idea."

"It's a little too late to have second thoughts, babe," Lester replied. "What's done is done."

Jane could hear the frustration in Lester's voice. He had been the one who was against involving his father from the beginning, and now that Jane was having second thoughts, she could understand how he might be feeling.

"You're right," Jane said, hoping to backtrack her fears. "This was the decision we made, and we will live with the consequences."

Lester kept his head down as he remained sitting on the edge of the cot. Jane walked over to him and sat next to him.

"Thank you for getting on board with this," Jane said. "I know it wasn't easy for you."

Lester rubbed his palms against his thighs. He exhaled and shook his head. "I just hope this works. Because I know how he gets when plans get changed."

Jane reached for her husband's hand and held it tightly. The door opened quickly, and Jane saw Danny standing in the doorway. She knew something was wrong just by the look on his face and the abruptness of his entry.

"There's a problem," Danny said.

Jane didn't waste any time as she got up to follow Danny out of the portable. Lester came as well, and when Danny brought them over to Marty Schwartz's place and they peered inside, she saw the man lying on the floor.

Jane quickly turned around and struggled to keep her voice down. "What the hell happened?"

Danny shook his head. "The guy just kept telling me that he had to kill him. I guess Marty was fighting back too hard."

Jane took a few steps as the twilight hours provided just enough glimpse for Jane to see the several blood-stains along Marty's stomach. The man was drenched in blood, and Jane doubted that this was an act of self-defense."

"He must've been stabbed a dozen times," Jane said.

Jane struggled to collect her thoughts, but she knew she needed to come up with something quickly. She realized that if Marty were here alone, it meant the girls hadn't been here, and because no one else had raised an alarm, they still have time to go enact their plan.

"We need to bring the prisoner here," Jane said.

"You mean we're still going through with this?" Lester asked.

"Nothing has changed," Jane answered. "So our guy got a little too overzealous. We can still salvage this. If we bring Abe here and then sound an alarm like we stumbled upon this, then it will be his word against ours. And nobody except for maybe the Rikers will believe what happened."

"Jane," Lester said, his eyes skeptical, "that's a bit of a stretch."

"We don't have any other options," Jane said. She turned to Danny. "Get Cole away from the prisoner, and then we'll go in and bust him out and bring him here. You've got five minutes. Go."

Danny didn't hesitate as he hurried out of Marty's portable. Jane ducked outside one more time to make sure they were still alone and then motioned for Lester to join her. But he remained frozen inside.

"Lester, we need to go," Jane said.

Lester couldn't tear his eyes away from Marty's body. He looked mesmerized by what he'd seen. "This is how it's going to be with him. It's always going to be extreme measures." He turned around to face his wife.

"Lester, let's go," Jane said, adding even more urgency.

"It's not too late for us to get out of this," Lester said. "We could leave here. You, me, and Danny and Gray. We could start over anywhere. I know we can."

It was a sweet sentiment, but Jane knew that Lester wasn't thinking logically. Everything they needed to survive was here. All they had to do now was hold on for the next ten minutes, and they could find themselves at the helm of this place.

"We're staying," Jane said. "We are all in now."

Lester was still hesitant, but he offered no more objections. He nodded and then followed Jane out of the portable. So far, it didn't seem as though anyone had seen them. And the fading light made it difficult to know who was who walking around.

The pair headed toward the main building and around the edge, making sure they could see the exit where Cole would be leaving with Danny. Jane became anxious the longer they went without seeing anyone, but she knew she had to keep her cool, so Lester remained calm.

Eventually, Jane watched as Cole hurried out of the main building. Whatever Danny had told Cole had worked, and then Jane and Lester hurried inside.

Once they were certain nobody else was inside the building, Jane and Lester hurried toward where the prisoner was being held. The keys were always nearby, and Jane grabbed them from the wall as they headed toward the prisoner's cell.

The door was open, as it usually was, and Jane saw the man lying on his cot. At first, she thought maybe he was sleeping, but when she stepped inside, he propped himself up on his elbows.

Jane wasn't sure who the prisoner hoped it would be to come and visit him, but the smile vanished from his face when he saw it was her.

"What do you want?" Abe asked.

Jane said nothing and knew they needed to act quickly if they were going to pull this off. She and Lester walked with authority toward Abe's cot. Lester kept the man still while Jane removed his handcuffs and left them dangling against the wall where they were connected.

"What's going on?" Abe asked, growing more concerned.

"Liz Riker wants to see you," Jane answered. "Let's go."

Lester was much bigger than Abe and was able to manhandle the prisoner as they walked out of the building.

"Why didn't she just come to see me?" Abe asked.

"You're not in a position to be asking questions," Jane answered.

They moved at a quick pace, Jane not wanting to stop to draw any attention to themselves. She knew that taking him out like this was a risk, but Buford's man had forced their hand.

When they neared Marty's portable, Jane was the first one up the steps and then opened the door as Lester shoved Abe inside.

The man tripped when he entered, falling headfirst into Marty's body. Abe freaked out for a minute and then stood up, now covered in Marty's blood.

"What the hell is this?" Abe asked.

Jane already had her weapon drawn and then tossed the bloodied knife that Buford's man had used to kill Marty at Abe's feet.

Abe stared down at the blade, then stared at Marty, and then finally realized what was happening. He shook his head. "I didn't do this."

"Maybe," Jane said. "Maybe not. We'll let the court of opinion handle that."

Abe clenched his fists at his side. "I doubt I'll be around to defend myself."

"No," Jane said, placing her finger on the trigger, "you won't." Jane was about to pull the trigger when she heard footsteps and a voice behind her.

"Marty? I know tonight was a setback, but—" Wendy Sutton stepped into the doorway and froze when she saw the scene unfolding in front of her. She stared at Marty's body the longest and then looked to Jane and Lester. "Oh my God."

Jane knew she needed to think quickly before Abe could poison the situation with the truth. "Thank God you're here, Wendy." She gestured to Abe. "We heard a disturbance at Marty's place and then came into find this."

"That's a lie," Abe said.

"Shut up!" Jane shouted.

"He did that?" Wendy asked. "You really are a cold-blooded monster!"

"Wendy," Jane said, trying to bring the women off the ledge. "Wendy, I need you to look at me now."

Wendy turned her tear-streaked face to Jane.

"Go get Liz," Jane said. "She needs to know what's happened. In fact, get everyone." Jane looked back at Abe. "It's time this man received the justice he deserves."

* * *

AFTER THE VOTE WAS OVER, Nancy knew there was going to be a conversation between herself and Mrs. Riker. She had caught the angry glares sent her way and knew that it was only a matter of time before Mrs. Riker spoke to her, so she decided to face up to it immediately.

Nancy walked over to Mrs. Riker's portable and waited for her to show up. She was more nervous than she'd ever been in her life, but she knew she had done the right thing. There was no question about that. She was more nervous about facing Mrs. Riker's disappointment. She had clearly gone against her wishes, and Nancy wasn't sure what kind of consequences lay ahead of her.

Lost in her own thoughts and worry, Nancy didn't notice Mrs. Riker approach until she was standing at the foot of the steps where Nancy had sat down.

"I didn't expect to find you here," Mrs. Riker said.

Nancy stood and cleared her throat. "I thought it best if you and I spoke sooner rather than later."

Mrs. Riker remained silent, and Nancy wasn't sure what kind of hell would rain down on her, but when Mrs. Riker sighed and slowly trudged up the steps to join Nancy by the door, she looked more exhausted than angry.

"Let's talk inside," Mrs. Riker said.

Nancy followed Mrs. Riker into the portable and remained standing while Mrs. Riker sat down on one of the beds and rubbed her face.

"I spoke to Gray," Nancy said. "I put the idea in his head to say what he did at the meeting."

"I figured as much," Mrs. Riker said, still rubbing her face.

"I understand if you're angry," Nancy said, "and I'm prepared to face whatever punishment you deem fit." She straightened up. "But I want to be clear that if I had the opportunity, I would do it all over again."

Mrs. Riker finally looked up at Nancy, her face red. "You really aren't the scared little girl who came here with us anymore, are you?" She stood and then walked over to Nancy. "I know you believe that what you did was the right thing to do, but you also need to under-stand the consequences of your actions."

"I told you I'm ready—"

"I'm not talking about some kind of punishment I would give you," Mrs. Riker said. "Which, for the record, I'm not."

Nancy frowned. "You're not?"

"No," Mrs. Riker answered as she returned to the cot and sat down. "Because the truth of the matter is you were right. If Gray hadn't spoken up, I don't think I would still be in charge."

Nancy was a little shocked. She hadn't expected Mrs. Riker to side with her. "Then, what do you mean by consequences?"

"You know Jane Percy pretty well by now," Mrs. Riker answered. "You don't think she's going to put together what happened tonight? She's not a forgiving woman, Nancy. And what you did will have conse-quences beyond this evening. Lines have been drawn. It's only a matter of time before—"

"Marty's dead!" Wendy rushed into the portable, shoulder-checking the door open as she caught her breath from the sprint to find them.

Mrs. Riker shot up from bed. "What?"

"The prisoner got out and killed him," Wendy answered. "You need to come over now!"

Wendy was out the door before Mrs. Riker or Nancy could gather any more information, but neither of them dawdled as they sprinted for Marty's portable.

A crowd had gathered outside Marty's portable. Everybody in the compound had shown up. And when Nancy saw Jane and Lester Percy at the top of the steps with Abe, who was covered in blood, she pushed through the crowd to rush to his aid, Mrs. Riker close behind.

"Let him go!" Nancy shouted.

"He's a murderer," Jane said. "Killed Marty in cold blood."

"I did no such thing—"

Lester jammed the butt of his rifle against Abe's back, knocking him to his knees. Nancy was about to jump forward, but Mrs. Riker held her back.

"This man needs to be served the justice he should have been given the moment he was brought here," Jane said, speaking to the crowd as much as she was to Mrs. Riker. "You and your husband have kept him alive for too long."

Nancy turned to Mrs. Riker, pleading. "She's lying. Abe wouldn't kill him. He was locked up!" She hated how much she sounded like a whiny teenager, but she couldn't help herself.

Mrs. Riker kept her cool despite the crowd behind them growing antsier and more upset the longer Abe didn't have a bullet in his head.

"If he's guilty, then he should stand trial," Mrs. Riker said.

"Trial?" Jane asked. "He killed one of our people!

Someone you vowed to protect! Why should he get the benefit of a trial?"

Nancy could tell that Jane had set an elaborate trap, and no matter what Mrs. Riker did, she was damned. If she didn't kill Abe, the crowd would turn against her. If she did kill Abe... then she would be murdering an innocent man.

"Hand him over, Jane," Mrs. Riker said, walking up the steps.

Jane Percy looked like she had no intention of handing over Abe, but Nancy was surprised when she shoved Abe forward and into Mrs. Riker's arms.

"No!" a voice from the crowd shouted, and Nancy turned to see Wendy Sutton pushing her way through the crowd. "He needs to pay!"

The other spectators gave her a wide berth, and as the people cleared, Nancy saw the pistol in her hand. Wendy walked right up to the edge of the steps, just out of arms' reach from Nancy, and then aimed the pistol at Abe.

"He needs to die!" Wendy shouted.

On instinct, Nancy raised her own weapon and aimed it at Wendy. "Drop the gun, now!"

The crowd gasped, and everyone stepped back but couldn't look away.

Mrs. Riker held up her hands and tried to calm the situation. "Everyone, relax," Mrs. Riker said.

Nancy kept a bead on Wendy, but all of the woman's attention was focused on Abe.

"You need to make a choice, Liz," Jane said. "You can either cozy up with the enemy and continue to protect him even after our people are murdered in their own beds, or you can do the right thing and kill him now."

Nancy felt the tears filling up in her eyes. She was burning hot with anger and then looked to Mrs. Riker and saw that she was actually considering it. "No. He didn't do anything. He's not a bad person!"

"He's a killer," Wendy said, sounding more like she was trying to convince herself. "He's just like those people who killed my Jeff!"

Everyone waited to hear what Mrs. Riker would say, and Nancy feared that she would give in. But when Mrs. Riker walked down the steps and stood in Nancy's line of fire, she started to cry.

"No," Nancy said.

"Lower the weapon, Nancy," Mrs. Riker said. "Please." Mrs. Riker was incredibly calm and collected, and when she gently placed her hand on the end of Nancy's rifle, it lowered. Mrs. Riker then turned to Wendy. "Put it down, Wendy."

Wendy Sutton was shaking uncontrollably. Her adrenaline was getting the better of her, and she looked wild, like a feral animal. "No," Wendy said.

"You can't kill him, Wendy," Mrs. Riker said. "That would make you no better than the people who killed your husband."

"Someone has to pay," Wendy said.

Mrs. Riker stepped in front of Wendy. "Put the gun down, Wendy."

Nancy and the rest of the crowd waited with bated breath. Nancy looked up at Abe and saw him still on his knees, looking right at her. He didn't look scared; instead, he looked almost peaceful.

"Move, Liz," Wendy said, gritting her teeth. "Now."

"I'm not going to move, Wendy," Liz said. "I'm not going to let you kill someone."

Nancy could do nothing but sit and wait, and just when she thought Wendy was going to pull the trigger, the woman lowered her weapon, gasping for air as if she had been holding her breath.

A collected sigh escaped the crowd, but the only person who wasn't relieved was Jane Percy.

"So you're just going to let him get away with it?" Jane asked. "He's a killer!"

"The only killer here is you," Nancy said.

Jane looked like she might shoot Nancy on the spot, but no action was taken.

Wendy was crying, shaking her head. "I'm sorry, Jeff. I'm so sorry."

Mrs. Riker slowly reached for the pistol in Wendy's hand, but just before she could reach it, Wendy jolted, stepping around Mrs. Riker to shoot Abe.

"No!" Nancy lunged, but she wasn't close enough.

She watched Mrs. Riker reach for the gun and then brought Wendy to the ground. The pair grappled for the weapon, and just as Nancy reached to help Mrs. Riker, the gun fired.

A few people screamed, but everyone froze. Both Wendy's and Mrs. Riker's faces were wide with shock. Nancy pulled Mrs. Riker back, checking for a gunshot wound but found none. The bullet had gone into Wendy's stomach, and she was bleeding.

"Liz shot her!" Jane shouted, capitalizing on the moment. "She killed one of us!"

Realizing the situation was a powder keg about to blow, Nancy pulled Mrs. Riker back, along with Abe, and retreated, keeping her gun aimed at Jane and Lester.

"They're traitors!" Jane shouted. "Traitors who don't belong here!"

Nancy kept a bead on Jane and knew she could kill her at that moment. But when Mrs. Riker squeezed Nancy's shoulder and whispered into her ear, "We need to grab my boys and leave," Nancy held back.

If they wanted to get out with their lives, then Nancy would have to wait a little longer before she shot Jane Percy.

he bombing seemed to last forever. Every blast caused the ground to tremble like the earth was going to crack open. Ben barely had time to rush to find cover before the first bombs dropped. He managed to find shelter beneath a thick piece of concrete that had survived the fires. But with the amount of ordinance that was dropping from above, Ben wasn't sure if the structure would hold.

The carnage Ben witnessed from beneath the covering was catastrophic. Soldiers scrambled to find anything that could withstand the bombs from disintegrating men into dust. Ben had thought he had seen real devastation from the fires that ravaged his home, but the carnage he witnessed, seeing pieces of men flung in different directions, was beyond anything he could have imagined.

A few of the explosions got close to where Ben had found shelter, but he escaped the brunt of the blast.

Once the explosions stopped, Ben could only hear the faint buzz of the primitive drones continuing their aimless flight forward. And once the drones faded, there were only the painful groans of the survivors.

Ben emerged from the concrete overhang and squinted in horror at the graveyard the bombs had left behind.

The army that had come to save them from a far less sophisticated enemy had been decimated by a clever tactic. No one, not even Ben, anticipated the ingenuity of these people. It had been their tragic flaw, and now they were on the brink of oblivion.

Ben started going to each body that he found and checked to see who was alive, who was struggling to stay that way, and who had already passed.

Most were dead, but eventually, Ben came across a young man who had a piece of shrapnel sticking in his stomach. He had blood in his mouth, and his eyes were bloodshot. He was struggling for breath, and when he saw Ben, he stretched out his hand, and it was all Ben could do to take hold of it and give the boy some comfort.

"It's... hard... to... breathe..." The boy gasped between each word, and despite the warm evening, his hand was cold as ice.

"It's all right," Ben said, trying to offer what comfort he could. "Just take it nice and slow. Breathe like me, in and then out." Ben did slow inhales, and then slow exhales, and watched as the young soldier struggled to follow along.

The kid couldn't have been older than eighteen, probably fresh out of boot camp, or perhaps he hadn't even finished and was mobilized to come here and join the fight.

Ben held onto the soldier until the last few breaths drained from him, and the boy became completely still. Ben continued to hold the boy's hand, and he couldn't help but wonder where his parents were and when and if they would ever learn of their son's fate.

"Ben!" Jackson weaved his way through the rubble. Dir and soot smeared his cheeks, which were red from exertion. "I can't believe you survived."

Ben kept his attention on the young boy now dead. How many other young men and women would die throughout this conflict? How much blood needed to be shed before people realized that this fight was pointless?

"Ben, we need to move," Jackson said. "The enemies are advancing to the front lines."

Ben gently laid the boy's hand down on his stomach and then folded the other one on top of it. Ben held the cold hands there for a moment before reaching up and closing the young man's eyes. "Be at peace now."

Ben stood, still staring down at the young man as Jackson grew more anxious.

"Ben, we need to go," Jackson said.

"Where's the device?" Ben asked.

"What?" Jackson answered.

Ben faced Jackson. "The piece of the nuclear device we brought here, where is it?"

Jackson gestured to the rubble that surrounded them. "Buried somewhere under here, I guess."

"We need to find it," Ben said. "We need to make sure it doesn't fall back into their hands."

"It's probably destroyed," Jackson said. "Half of our forces are gone. They are barely holding back the bastards at the frontline as it is. They must've known we were coming and planned to arrive here earlier than we expected."

"All the more reason to get the device," Ben said. "If they knew the military was already here, they also probably know about the device we stole. They came here because they want it back."

Gunfire erupted nearby, and both Ben and Jackson reached for their weapons. They saw a small unit of American soldiers retreating from the advancement of around fifty enemy combatants. In the span of thirty seconds, Ben watched as at least three of the American soldiers were killed while their comrades struggled to bring their bodies back to a safe spot.

"We need to move," Jackson said.

Ben knew they couldn't take on all of those soldiers, but they might be able to salvage all this by making sure the device needed to complete the nuclear bomb didn't fall back into the enemy's possession.

Ben and Jackson headed back into the strip mall where the command had been set up. Ben wasn't sure what to expect to find, but he was surprised when he found the commanders still around the table, trying to strategize on how to pull everyone out.

Before Ben could speak, a young soldier darted past Ben and Jackson and into the tent.

"General! They've gotten past our second lines. Everyone is in full retreat." The young soldier was out of breath, and he was covered in dust from the bombs.

General McGuire looked at the map and then frowned. "Pull everyone back to the checkpoint. Grab as many wounded as we can carry. Make sure everyone makes it back."

"Yes, sir!" The boy saluted, still maintaining decorum even in all of this chaos. He darted past Ben and Jackson.

"Sir, we think the enemy is also making a play for the device we brought back," Jackson said.

McGuire looked away from the map and to the duffle bag, Ben and Jackson had brought in. "So much fuss over a little piece of a machine."

"Sir," Ben said, stepping forward, "we need to get that thing out of here."

McGuire walked back to the table and scribbled something on a piece of paper, and then handed it to Jackson. "There is another unit heading down from the north. It's small, definitely not enough to handle the fight that's heading our way, but if you can get to them before they arrive here and give them the device, they can get it back to DC before they run into the same trouble we had here." The general handed Ben the duffel bag. "It's imperative they do not recover this again."

Even though Ben understood how important this was, he didn't want to leave his family again for another mission.

"Sir, my family is still at a compound nearby," Ben said. "If you could send over a unit to grab them and bring them here before the enemy finds them, I would be incredibly grateful."

Ben knew it was a tough task for the general, considering the situation everybody found themselves in, but he had to try. Because if the general wouldn't send somebody, then Ben would go back himself. And Jackson would have to take this device to the unit alone.

"I'll send over unit if you give me their coordinates," McGuire said.

Ben sighed in relief. "Thank you, sir."

Once Ben relayed the compound's coordinates, the general dismissed them. Before they left, Jackson turned back to McGuire. "Sir, we will turn this around."

"You bet your ass we will, Colonel," McGuire said. "Good luck to both of you."

With their mission clear, Ben and Jackson hurried out of the building as the enemy forces started inched closer. Asheville had once again transformed into a war zone. And Ben could only hope to survive like he had done before.

* * *

THE SOLDIERS never saw what was coming. Mark and his unit had taken them completely by surprise. The bombs had delivered a devastating blow to their numbers, and as his men advanced through the city, it was like shooting fish in a barrel.

But while Mark was in the fight, his mind was across the river. The Supreme Leader's words echoed in his mind, and Mark feared to finally purge himself of what remained of his past.

One of the scouts ahead returned and gave Mark the report that the army was in full retreat. From a battle standpoint, the fight was a success, but Mark also needed to recover the piece of the nuclear device that had been taken. He was certain the military was in possession of it. He just had to find it.

Mark called for his best scouts to come with him. He told them about the device they needed to recover. He then handed command over to the next man in line, with only one order: no survivors.

Mark figured that the military would try to toss the nuclear device to a small unit to send out of the warzone. If that were the case, the most likely scenario was one or two guys moving discreetly away from the city. They wouldn't want to go backward, and they couldn't go forward, so the options were north or south. Mark chose north.

It was odd walking through the charred remains of the city he had grown up in as a kid. There were several stores he passed he remembered visiting with his parents and his brother. The memories were distorted and fuzzy, much like the physical places themselves. It was almost like those memories were nothing but a dream. A dream that he wasn't even sure was his own anymore.

Mark moved with the same level of stealth and quiet as he did whenever he was hunting. He was so silent that even the birds pecking at bits of trash and dust didn't notice and passed by within a few feet. It was a skill he had honed in the mountains outside of the city. And it was a skill that had served him well in war.

Eventually, Mark heard two sets of boots on the next street over hitting the pavement. Their frantic pace suggested they were in a hurry. And Mark hastened his own pace to catch up to get a good look at who was running.

Mark was certain that whoever it was did not belong to his own unit, which meant these were either deserters from the main army or the carriers of the device Mark sought.

It took a minute for Mark to find a cut through to get him onto the next street, and by the time that happened, the pair had darted down another side street to the north after their current path was blocked by a fallen building.

Mark double-timed it as he chased them. He wasn't about to let them get away, and when he turned onto the next street, he had a good line of sight on them. But it wasn't until Mark placed his eyes through the scope that he recognized one of the men on the run.

It was his brother, Ben.

22

*N*ancy never dropped her weapon as she guarded Mrs. Riker's retreat to her portable. She found Sarah and the boys still inside, along with Ali and Marty's two girls. The pair were now orphans, and Mrs. Riker had no intention of leaving them here.

"We need to pack, and we need to go, now." Liz had already packed go-bags when they arrived here in case of just such an emergency. All they had to do was get everyone together. "Have you seen your father and aunt?"

Sarah started helping the boys get their packs on. "No, what's going on?"

"The Percys have taken over," Nancy answered.

"What?" Sarah asked, and then she noticed Abe for the first time. "What the hell is he doing here?"

"He's coming with us, too," Liz answered.

"Assuming he doesn't cause any trouble." She looked at him with a very skeptical eye.

"No problem here, ma'am," Abe said.

"Good." Liz loaded a magazine into her pistol and then slung the rifle over her shoulder. "Everyone ready? Let's go."

Liz tasked Sarah with keeping the kids close, and the moment they stepped outside the portable, Liz heard the sound of dissent coming from the rest of the community. Jane had riled up everyone, and now they were out for blood.

They moved toward Cole and Rachel's portable, not bothering to knock on the door before Liz entered. Thankfully, she found them fully clothed, though it didn't look like they were going to stay that way for long.

"Liz!" Rachel said, climbing off of Cole's lap. "What the hell are you doing?"

"We're leaving," Liz said. "Put on good walking shoes. Cole, get your rifle. Now!" she barked the order, and the pair snapped to attention.

"What's going on out there?" Cole asked.

Liz could have shot him then and there for leaving his post. He was as unreliable as he'd always been, chasing tail instead of doing his job. "We're covering up your mistake. Let's go."

By the time the pair left the portable, Liz saw the mob heading toward them. She quickly changed course and headed for the back gate, but that path was also blocked by Lester and Danny Percy. They were surrounded.

"Give him up, Liz!" Jane shouted. "We don't want to hurt you or the kids. Just hand over the terrorist."

Nancy was the first to step forward, gun up, and aimed. "Go to hell!"

Liz knew that the inflammatory remark wasn't going to help, and while she appreciated Nancy's fervor to defend an innocent man, Liz wasn't about to put Abe's life ahead of her children's. But she knew how Jane Percy worked. You gave her an inch, and she'd run for the whole mile.

"We're going to leave," Liz said. "All of us."

Liz noted that the crowd behind Jane was now mostly armed. Even Kurt and Tony. When she saw them, she didn't expect it to hurt that bad

"Just let him go, Liz," Tony said, his voice pleading. "You know he deserves exactly what's coming to him."

"Does he?" Liz asked. "Because last time I checked, you weren't a judge, Tony. And this wasn't a court of law!" She raised her voice, challenging the others and their way of thinking. "No man deserves to be killed without due process. And this man hasn't had his day in court."

"There are no more courts!" Jane barked. "No more law. No more military. We're on our own, and if we don't deal with traitors like him now, then we're going to be stuck cleaning up messes for the rest of our lives." Jane stepped closer, raising her gun. "I don't want this to end in bloodshed, Liz. For the sake of your family, give him up."

Liz knew she was caught between a rock and a hard place, but before she could answer, Abe stepped forward. "It's fine." He gestured for her to lower her weapon. "You go. I'll stay here."

"No," Nancy said.

"They'll kill you," Liz said.

Abe didn't have the look of a man who feared death but instead welcomed it. Whatever pain he was dealing with must have been extreme to go to this level. "Your family should not die because of me," Abe said. "I knew I would have to face the consequences of my actions one day. Turns out that day is now."

Liz admired the man's courage. But even after Abe turned himself over, it wouldn't guarantee Liz and her family safe passage. She needed to make sure they were out and away from this place before that happened. Abe was her only bargaining chip.

"We'll do the pass off at the gate," Liz said. "You get him, and then my family leaves. Deal?"

Liz wasn't sure if Jane would go for the deal or not, but she could see the woman's wheels turning. She was considering just killing them all here, but then she would lose what small amount of clout she had with the rest of the community.

"Deal," Jane answered.

The walk over to the front gate was tense. Nobody

lowered their weapons as they moved, and Abe stayed with Liz and Nancy the entire way.

Liz struggled to keep her attention focused, but she knew that keeping her eyes on Jane was the most important part. The others wouldn't make a move unless she did.

When they reached the front gate, Liz made sure that her family was well into the woods before the handoff happened. But when she looked to her left, she saw that Nancy was still nearby. She had her rifle aimed at Jane with a look of pure hatred in her eye.

"Nancy," Liz said. "You need to lower your weapon and join the others in the forest."

It was hard to tell now in the darkness, but Liz believed Nancy had tears running down her cheeks. "They can't have him. He didn't kill anyone."

Liz was not sure what else she could say to Nancy to convince her to lower the weapon. But thankfully, Abe walked over to her and stood in front of the rifle.

"You need to go," Abe said.

"Not without you," Nancy said.

Abe lowered Nancy's rifle and then stepped closer to her. Liz had noticed the two becoming close, but it was obvious to her now what was going on. They had come to care for one another.

"I got myself into this business," Abe said. "I'm not going to let anyone else die because of me. Somebody once told me that I needed to take responsibility for what I've done. Let me do that now."

Nancy stood there in shock, and it wasn't until Liz walked over and steered her toward the forest that she moved.

"Go," Liz said, gently nudging Nancy toward the tree line. "Keep my kids safe."

Liz hoped the sense of duty would allow Nancy to focus on something other than losing a friend, and she reluctantly headed toward the woods.

Liz looked to Abe and knew that leaving him was condemning him to death. But she reminded herself that he had chosen this life and that he was volunteering to make things right. Not to mention this was keeping her family alive.

"Thank you," Liz said. She opened her mouth to say more, but nothing else came.

Abe nodded. "Tell your husband thank you for listening to me."

"I will." Liz stepped back and then looked to Jane Percy and the wolves that surrounded her, all of them licking their chops at their fresh meat.

"Lester," Jane said. "Go and grab him."

Lester stepped toward Abe, but he only made it halfway before a gunshot caused everybody to freeze.

Jane immediately drew her weapon and aimed it at Liz, and Liz did the same to Jane.

"Who fired that shot!" Jane shouted.

"It wasn't me!" Liz said, and then she turned back to the forest line where Nancy had stopped after the gunshot. "Nancy?"

"Not me!" Nancy shouted.

Liz looked into the crowd, trying to see who had the smoking gun and what they could have been shooting at? Because no one, not even Abe, had been shot.

"Let him go, Mom!" The voice shouted from the tower belonged to Gray Percy. He had his rifle aimed at the crowd below. "I have my bead on everyone. Abe doesn't leave here, and I start taking you out one at a time!"

Liz couldn't believe the extent that Gray was going to defy his mother. But even though Gray was trying to help, he could be making a sensitive situation worse.

"Gray!" Jane said, shouting up to the tower. "You drop that weapon and come down here right now!"

Jane's voice was a mixture of anger and pain. Liz imagined it was very hurtful for a woman like Jane, who valued family above all, to have her own son spit in her face in such a public forum. Twice in one day, no less.

"It's over, Mom," Gray said. "I'm not letting this go."

The stalemate was back on, and Liz didn't want to be part of this anymore. But she saw that Abe had a flicker of hope now that there was a chance for him to escape. Liz might be able to use this to her advantage.

"Jane," Liz said. "Just let him go. It's not worth it. You have the compound and everything else. You've won."

Liz knew the kind of person that Jane was. She was

a vengeful woman, and once she had set her mind to something, there was nothing that was going to stop her from accomplishing it. It was the reason Liz had been so hesitant to welcome them into the compound in the first place. And now she was about to lose everything.

"Lester," Jane said, her voice hollow and dry, "take him."

Liz saw the hesitation on Lester's face as he looked from the tower where his son was located to Abe, who was now standing next to Liz. He wasn't sure if his own son would shoot him or not, but he had never refused an order from his wife.

Lester stepped forward, and Gray fired another gunshot, and this time he didn't stop shooting. After that, all hell broke loose, and Liz grabbed hold of Abe, and the pair sprinted toward the woods.

Liz fired behind her, her shots meant to scatter and not actually hit anyone. Despite being betrayed by some of her closest friends, Liz didn't want anyone's life on her conscience.

When Liz reached the woods, she instructed everybody to keep running. The forest and the darkness would be their friend, and with Gray continuing to fire from the tower, preventing anyone from following, Liz knew they had a little time. So long as they could get to the river and cross before Jane got to Gray, they might be able to survive.

23

$\mathcal{T}$he sound of gunshots echoed behind them, and Ben wondered how long the military would be able to hold off the enemy's advancement. He couldn't imagine the enemy would continue to chase them past the city. Once they had secured Asheville, it would be the perfect place to set up camp. And it would also be incredibly close to Ben's family, and he had no intention of keeping them around.

"Do you think the general will keep his word?" Ben asked.

Jackson was huffing from the effort, and Ben figured the man was fatigued. Hell, Ben was barely able to keep moving forward, either. But the lives of the entire country were in Ben and Jackson's hands. If they didn't get this device to the right people, if it fell into the wrong hands, then the enemy would be one step closer to nuclear capabilities.

"The fighting isn't even anywhere close to your compound," Jackson said, attempting to sound reassuring. "They are not even in harm's way. But the general will keep his word."

"I know," Ben said, "but in my experience, trouble seems to always find me."

"I think you're being paranoid—"

The gunshot thundered from somewhere behind him, and Ben watched as Jackson took a bullet in the back and was flattened to the ground.

Ben glanced behind him to see where the shooter was positioned. But in the darkness, it was difficult to see anything.

Ben hurried toward a car for cover as more gunfire chased him behind the vehicle. Once he was safe, he located Jackson in the road. He waited a moment and caught his breath, and then he sprinted out to Jackson and pulled him back to safety, chased by more gunfire.

"Jackson?" Ben asked. "Hey, can you hear me?"

Ben carefully rolled Jackson onto his back just to see if the man was still breathing and then sighed with relief when he saw Jackson was still alive.

"How bad is it?" Jackson asked, clenching his teeth. "Because it feels like it's pretty bad."

Ben checked for an exit wound on the front shoulder and found it just below the collarbone on his right side. "It looks like the bullet went through. But it might have hit the top half of your right lung. Is it difficult to breathe?"

"It's not easy," Jackson answered.

Another gunshot ricocheted off the passenger car door to their left, and Ben ducked lower.

"We're sitting ducks out here," Jackson said, and then he forced himself to roll onto his side. "We need to move."

"You need to take it easy," Ben said. "We'll find some shelter nearby—"

"There isn't any time for that," Jackson said as he forced himself to stand. "You need to get the duffle bag to the unit." He reached for the bag with the device and then shoved it into Ben's arms. "Go. I'll hold him off."

Ben knew that Jackson was in no shape or condition to fight, but he also recognized the importance of what they were trying to do. The mission superseded his own life; that was the mandate of the soldier.

"Go," Jackson said, positioning himself under the cover by the door. "At the very least, I can buy you some time."

Ben had already sacrificed so much, and he knew that Jackson's sacrifice here was a gift. He needed to go, and he needed to do it now.

"Go!" Jackson shouted, growing angry now that Ben continued to defy him. "Before I change my mind and make you stay!"

Ben nodded. Another gunshot echoed, and Ben could have sworn he felt the bullet rush past his ear, but he knew that he was just being paranoid. He double-timed it on his way out of the city, but his bad luck only continued.

A hot searing pain exploded in his left calf, and Ben collapsed as he landed hard across the asphalt. When Ben hit the pavement, he lost his grip on the duffle bag, and it crashed to the ground. It sounded as though it might have broken when it landed, but that was the least of Ben's worries.

A pain traveled up his arm, and he glanced down to find that his sleeve had been completely ripped up; there was road rash down his arm. His left calf was numb, and the cool night air stung the bullet wound.

With the gunmen no doubt heading down toward him to finish the job and also collect the device, Ben reached for the duffle bag and forced himself to stand. Even though his arm and leg were on fire with pain, he managed to shuffle forward, and he had his pistol at the ready should the shooter get too close.

Ben limped forward, moving at a glacier's pace, hoping to escape this place with his life. But the darkness falling around him made it difficult to see, and his vision was starting to blur from the pain.

The next gunshot forced Ben to scramble behind a column of concrete next to the road. It had once held up an arch for a decorative entryway into a cluster of shops that were now nothing but burnt skeletons of their former selves.

Ben dropped the duffel bag, and he had to use both hands to grip the pistol. He used the injured arm as the trigger, and he didn't think it was strong enough to hold and aim the pistol and handle recoil if he were to fire.

Ben carefully peered around the edge of the pillar, unsure of what kind of scope the shooter had at his disposal or how skilled of a shooter he was dealing with. Ben hated that his eyes adjusted to the darkness, and he looked for any shapes that were moving toward down the road.

There was a brief exchange of gunfire, several rounds, and Ben assumed that was Jackson's final stand. He knew the colonel was a formidable fighter, but he was injured, and the shooter that was tracking them had the element of surprise still on his side.

And then whatever hope that Ben was holding out for Jackson ended as another bullet struck the column Ben was using as cover. Ben fired off two rounds just to let the shooter knew he was still alive. But after Ben fired his weapon, he knew he was in no condition to hold his own. His best survival tactic now was evasion.

Ben searched for the nearest escape route and knew that while heading through some of the old, crumbling buildings was dangerous considering that they could collapse at any moment, he couldn't hold his current position.

Head pounding from the long day and the pain in his arm and his calf, Ben was distracted. And his frazzled mind missed the footsteps that had managed to sneak up behind him.

"That's far enough, Ben," Mark said.

Ben felt the end of Mark's rifle barrel nudge the back of his head, and he turned around to find his brother with a gun aimed at him.

"I knew you'd come back," Ben said. "You just couldn't let my family alone."

Mark remained stoic but steady. "I came to finish a job." He glanced down at the duffle bag before returning his attention to Ben. "Is that the device?"

Ben shook his head. "Just let me go, Mark. Do you really think the people you've sided with should have a nuclear bomb?"

"Open it up," Mark said. "But first, toss your pistol over there."

Ben did as he was told, and once the weapon was discarded, Ben opened the duffle bag. He wasn't sure how this device was supposed to be operated or if the device was broken or not, but Mark seemed satisfied with the contents inside.

"Push it toward me," Mark said.

Again, Ben followed the instructions. Once Mark had the duffel bag in his possession, he stepped backward, keeping the rifle aimed at Ben.

"Don't do this, Mark," Ben said. "If the organization you're with keeps getting their way, then the world as we know it will end. You know that this is wrong. I know you do."

Even though it was dark, Ben saw the conflict on his brother's face. He had always been somebody who wanted to fight for a cause. But Ben had never thought his brother would pick a cause that was so vile and dangerous.

"I know that you think that you have the moral high ground in this," Mark said. "But the world you're so quick to defend discarded us. After our parents were killed, there was nobody to help us, no justice. I was still a kid myself, and I wasn't in any condition to take care of you."

"All I'm hearing is that you were the one to discard me," Ben said. "Is that what you're here to do now? Again?"

"History does tend to repeat itself," Mark answered. "That's exactly what the people I am fighting with are trying to stop. We want to create a world where all of the mistakes we made are completely erased."

"And you think the best way to erase those mistakes is to set off a nuclear bomb, killing more of your countrymen?" Ben asked. "How many innocent people have to die? Because I can promise you that this trajectory that you're on won't leave a world left for you to rebuild."

Ben knew that somewhere beneath all of the propaganda that these people had shoved into Mark's head was the man who used to take him fishing. The brother who would sneak his dessert in the middle of the night after his parents had denied him when he didn't finish his dinner. He desperately wanted to reach his brother, but Mark had to take the first step.

"Come with me," Ben said. "The knowledge that you have about this organization could help bring an end to so much violence." Ben gestured to the city around them. "Look what happened to our home. Despite how much you say you hate this place, you mean to tell me that seeing it this way doesn't affect you at all?"

"I cannot be swayed," Mark said. "I have purged myself of all the things in my past that could cause me to fall back into old habits. I am not your brother anymore."

Ben could believe what he was hearing. Of course, he had cursed his brother for a very long time after what hc did, but deep down, he always wanted them to reconcile, and despite all of the anger he felt toward Mark, he knew he wanted to rekindle that connection.

But it seemed that Mark had no desire to do that.

"You've severed every connection?" Ben asked. "What about me, Mark? You had a chance to kill me, to kill my family the last time you were here when you tracked us from Charlotte. But you didn't. Why?"

Mark's face twitched, and Ben knew his brother was barely holding it together. Beneath that stoic gaze was a storm of emotion begging to be released.

"I can tell that you don't believe every single piece of information those people told you," Ben said. "Come home, Mark. Come back to your real family. Or have you forgotten what your family looks like?"

A single tear fell from Mark and rolled down to the thick scruff of his beard. Ben knew he had only seen his brother cry a few times in his life. Each was a significant moment for both of them.

"You're not beyond saving," Ben said. "No matter what kind of things you've done or what you are afraid the consequences might be, you are strong enough to come back."

"There is no coming back from this," Mark said. "Not after this."

"What are you talking about?" Ben asked. "There's still time. Give up this ludicrous fight and come with me. I know you don't want to do this. I can see it in your eyes, and you must feel it in your heart."

Mark shook his head. "You're right that I don't want to do this. But there is one last connection that I need to sever."

Ben realized what Mark was trying to say. "Mark, don't do this."

"I have to be fully committed," Mark said. "The night is long. But the dawn is bright."

Ben couldn't believe his brother would shoot to kill, not after all of this time. But when he stared a little closer into Mark's eyes, he knew he wasn't looking at his brother anymore. It was a stranger in front of him now.

"Mark—"

The gunshot was loud, and then the next thing Ben remembered was looking up at the stars. There was a coldness washing over him, and he became very still and calm. When Mark stepped over him, staring down at Ben, he was convinced this would be the last time he saw his brother. This would be the last time he saw the night sky.

"Goodbye, Ben." Mark picked up the duffle bag and then walked away.

Ben lay there, unable to move, his mind jumping between different memories. But the last one he landed on before he fell unconscious was before all of this had started. It was the morning of the EMP, and he and the boys, along with Liz, had just video chatted with Sarah. Everyone was smiling and laughing, and it ended with Connor spraying the video screen with whipped cream because Sarah had done the same to hers.

That had been a good morning. That had been a day to remember. The world was right that day, and at that moment, Ben didn't believe anything could ever ruin it. If that was his last memory, he was thankful to have it.

24

---

*T*he moment after the Rikers descended into the forest and Gray had finished shooting, Jane hurried up the tower to confront her son. She was so enraged by the time she reached the top that when she saw Gray standing there with his rifle at the side, she already had her own weapon aimed at him with her finger on the trigger.

Jane hated herself for wanting to pull it. She hated herself for even thinking about it. Gray was her own flesh and blood, but he had turned against her.

"Why?" Jane asked. "Why are you doing this to your family?"

She hadn't meant to sound so distressed, but Jane couldn't hide the truth in her voice. She had always worn her heart on her sleeve. When people accused her of being too cold, she always thought it was funny because she was just the opposite. She felt everything, and her emotions were difficult to keep in check.

Gray set the rifle down, leaning it up against the railing. He looked at his mother, defiant even now, and tilted his chin up. "I won't be a pawn in your game. My conscience is clean."

Jane lowered her rifle and crossed the platform to her son. "Your conscious is clean? Clean from what? From betraying your family? From letting a man who should have been hung for what he did to this world? Exactly what moral high ground are you taking here, Gray?"

It was obvious to Jane that her son had regrets. She could read the signs on his face, even though he was convinced he had none.

"What you did," Jane said, "will haunt you for the rest of your days." She turned to leave and made it to the stairs before Gray spoke again.

"The only thing that will haunt me is the fact that you're my mother," Gray said.

Jane paused, and she felt her heart crack at her son's words. But she quickly filled that crack with anger, and she moved on. "We will talk about this later." She didn't have time to deal with her son's righteous cause because she still had a group of people who needed to have their fears quelled.

Lester and Danny were at the bottom of the stairs when she arrived, and she saw that Lester wanted to go up and give the boy a beating, but Jane placed her hand on his chest and shook her head.

"Not now," Jane said. "We have other things to worry about."

Jane turned her attention to the crowd of people that had chosen to follow her. From what she had seen, only the Riker's immediate family followed them out of the place. Ben's firefighter family had chosen to stay behind. Jane was always amazed at the power modern amenities could offer. They chose shelter and supplies over old friends. They were Jane's kind of people, after all.

"Why was your son shooting at us?" Kurt Johnson asked.

"He was shooting at his father," Jane answered, clarifying the reason. "And it was a misunderstanding."

"Hell of a misunderstanding," Tony Kipper replied.

Jane figured the firefighters would cause the most trouble if they chose to stay behind, but it was clear Jane was now in charge, and she needed to set the tone of her leadership immediately.

"It's been a night of misunderstandings, wouldn't you say?" Jane asked, taunting both Kurt and Tony over the fact that they had been willing to let their close friends hang out to dry in order to save their own families. "After all, everybody thought Liz Riker was here to protect us and not help murderous traitors. And yet we find ourselves with Liz and her family gone and all of us still here."

Jane stepped between Tony and Kurt and entered the cluster of people who had gathered around. She wanted to insert herself into the group so people could see she wasn't afraid.

"The fate of our families now rests in our hands," Jane said. "I know that not everyone here voted for me. But I hope that we can all agree now that I'm still the best choice for us moving forward. I am a survivor, and I am a fighter, and I will not put the needs of myself before the needs of our community. I will do everything in my power to keep us safe and make sure something like what happened today never happens again."

Jane took a moment to look everyone in the eye and remained silent to let her words resonate amongst the crowd. She hoped her speech would reach everyone, but she was prepared to use her weapon if it came to violence because after everything she'd done, she wasn't about to lose this place.

Eventually, a woman stepped from the crowd and joined Jane in the circle. Jane recognized her as the nurse from the women's clinic. She was a short, heavyset Latina woman, but she was about the same height as Jane.

The pair of women locked eyes, and then the woman turned to the rest of the crowd. "She stayed when Liz Riker ran away. If that doesn't speak to her level of commitment to this place and to us, then I don't know what does." She faced Jane again and shook her hand. "Actions always speak louder than words."

Jane smiled as mild-mannered applause broke out around her. "Yes, they do," Jane said.

* * *

MARK WALKED through the small strip mall where the army had set their command tent. They had retreated out of the city and were heading northwest, according to some of Mark's scouts. The terrain was making it difficult, though, for their men to retain the upper hand, and Mark had called off the pursuit.

The military could afford to lose men, but Mark knew they still needed every fighter they could get for the future of their cause.

Mark placed the duffel bag with the piece of the nuclear device on the table. He opened it and examined the machinery. He wasn't sure if it was damaged or not, but he hoped the few scientists and engineers they still had working for them would be able to confirm if it were still operational.

And while Mark knew that he should be more concerned about the condition of the device, the only thing he could think about was the image of his brother lying in the street.

Mark hadn't checked for a pulse, but there was so much blood and no one around to help him, there was no chance of survival.

Ben was dead.

Ever since Mark was reunited with Ben on their

last encounter, he knew that it was unavoidable that they would meet again. Ben had always been strong-willed, even as a child. It was one of the reasons it was so difficult for Mark to try to raise him by himself.

But even though Mark saw all this coming, it didn't prepare him for the eventuality. He felt completely numb after pulling the trigger. He had killed the final piece of himself linked to a forgotten past.

The supreme leader had always spoken of purging yourself of anything and everything that would prevent you from accomplishing the mission. In order to create real change, a person needed to be absolute.

Mark had always thought there was something pure in the absolute. But now that he stood on that same platform, he was beginning to think differently. If his decision was right, then why did he feel so miserable? If their cause was so just, then why did he feel as though he had completely forsaken himself? He was supposed to be happy now. Or at the very least at peace.

"Sir?" One of Mark's men stood in the entrance to the old command tent. "The supreme leader is here to see you."

Mark spun around, surprised. "He's here?"

The young fighter looked as nervous as Mark felt. "Yes, sir. He wanted to come to see our progress. Should I send him to see you?"

"No," Mark answered quickly, and then he picked up the duffle bag. "I will go to him."

Mark walked quickly through the camp. His men had already set up a perimeter and secured the city. It would act as a good foothold for repelling the eastern wave of troops that were heading their way. Of course, now that they had recovered the stolen piece of the bomb, Mark wasn't even sure if the supreme leader wanted them to stay.

The supreme leader walked through the camp to raucous cheers. It was as though the men believed the supreme leader was with them the entire fight. That was the kind of hold that he held over everybody in the organization. It was the same type of energy and charisma that had pulled Mark into all of this ten years ago.

"Marcus," the supreme leader said, opening his arms and walking toward Mark with a smile on his face. "You and our men have done tremendous work."

"Thank you, sir," Mark said, and then he raised a duffel bag. handing it to the supreme leader. "I don't know if it's operational, but I managed to bring it back."

The supreme leader took the duffle bag from Mark as if it were a sacred token. He removed the machinery from inside and couldn't wipe the smile from his face as he stared at it.

"And so our dream lives on," the supreme leader said and then looked up at Mark. "You will be remembered as one of the greatest generals of our time. History will never forget your name, Marcus."

Mark's voice caught in his throat when he replied. "Thank you, sir."

The supreme leader inched closer and lowered his voice. "And have you purged yourself of that troublesome past?"

Mark nodded. "Yes, sir. That won't be a problem anymore."

"Good," the supreme leader said, and then he smiled, flashing those stained, yellow teeth. "I'm so proud of you." He patted Mark on the shoulder, like grandfather dismissing a little boy.

The supreme leader turned to face the rest of the men and then raised the device high above his head. The men cheered, erupting into another raucous frenzy as though the supreme leader was raising the head of their enemies.

But while Mark should have been reveling in their victory along with the rest of the men in his unit, all Mark could think about was his brother rotting in the street. He knew he should at least go back and bury the body, but he didn't think he had the strength. And for what came next in their crusade, Mark would need every ounce of his strength if he wanted to survive.

THE VOICES SOUNDED echoey and like they were underwater. Whatever they said was nonsensical, and the volume faded in and out. But then a voice crept through, a voice that was recognizable and comforting and didn't seem possible.

"Ben?"

Ben cracked his eyes open, and he saw a blurred vision of Liz. She smiled at him, and he could tell that she'd been crying.

"Oh, thank God." Liz collapsed onto Ben's arm, and she cried.

Ben knew he should have been relieved at the sight of his wife, but he couldn't comprehend how he was even alive.

"I told you he was hard to kill."

Ben looked to his left and saw Colonel Jackson in a bed next to him. He had a bandage over his shoulder where he had been shot.

"I dragged you out," Jackson said, seeing the confusion on Ben's face. "Well, I managed to crawl over to you, and then some of our guys came and dragged us both out. But I got there in time to stop the bleeding. You're welcome."

Ben winced and then rolled his head back to face his wife. His mind was still swimming in confusion. "Where are we?"

"A military camp," Liz answered, wiping her eyes.

"They came and got you?" Ben asked, remembering the general sending one of his men to the compound, but then Liz shook her head.

"We had to leave," Liz said. "The Percys took it over. The kids are fine. Cole and Rachel are with us. And

Nancy and Abe came with us, too. But…" She trailed off, shaking her head. "But everyone else stayed behind."

It was a lot for Ben to take in in his current state. But then he remembered that he had lost the device to the bomb, and it was now in the enemy's possession.

"Ben?" Liz asked. "I'm so sorry."

Ben reached for his wife's hand and mustered enough strength to give her a reassuring squeeze. And while it was difficult to lose the compound, the loss paled in comparison to Ben's failed mission. Because now the enemy was one step closer to creating a nuclear bomb. And God only knew what they planned to do with it.

Made in the USA
Middletown, DE
12 March 2023